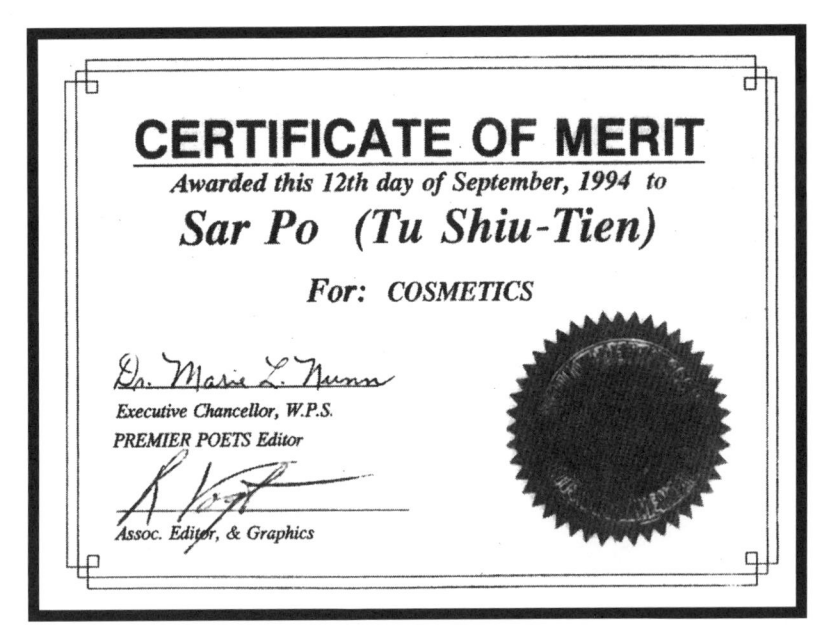

CERTIFICATE OF MERIT

Awarded this 12th day of September, 1994 to

Sar Po (Tu Shiu-Tien)

For: COSMETICS

Dr. Marie L. Nunn
Executive Chancellor, W.P.S.
PREMIER POETS Editor

Assoc. Editor, & Graphics

美國的國際詩人會頒給沙白的詩「化粧(Cosmetics)」卓越獎

The International Society of Poets

— *hereby awards* —

Sar Po (Tu Shiu-tien)

The International Poet of Merit Award

nineteen ninety-five

Elizabeth Barnes
President

沙白（涂秀田）1995年榮獲國際詩人獎

唱歌的河流
Singing Rivers

著／沙　白 Sar Po
譯／陳靖奇教授 Prof Ching-chi Chen, Ph.d.
圖／莊敏蓉・劉淑威・張俊成・秦麗美・許博文

Contents 目錄

中文	English	頁碼
黃榮村序（考試院院長／前中國醫藥大學校長）		6
毛連塭局長序	Foreword-By Mao Lianwen	8
苗栗縣長徐耀昌	Foreword-By Yao-chang Hsu	10
南投縣長林明溱	Mingzhen Lin	12
澎湖縣長賴峰偉	Feng-wui Lai	14
林良理事長序	Foreword by Lin Liang	16
自序	Preface	22
唱歌的河流	A Singing River	28
石頭	Pebbles	30
春天	Springtime	32
苦和樂	Bitterness and Sweetness	34
球	A Ball	36
母雞	The Hen	38
小狗	Puppies	40
小公雞	Little Cocks	42
豬	Piggies	44
毛毛蟲	A Caterpillar	46
植物園	The Botanical Garden	48
腳踏車	The Bicycle	50
大冬瓜	The Big Winter Melon	52
蠟燭	The Candle	54

中文	English	頁碼
鏡子	The Mirror	56
小鳥的歌聲	The Chirping of Little Birds	58 / 60
鳥的快樂	Happy Birds	60 / 62
美麗的世界	The Beautiful World	62 / 64
夢	A Dream	64 / 66
月餅	Mooncakes	66 / 68
我是一隻蠟燭	If I were a Candle	68 / 72
一朵美麗的花	A Beautiful Flower	72 / 74
初秋的落葉	Fallen Leaves in Early Autumn	74 / 76
時間	Time	76 / 78
日夜	Day and Night	78 / 80
夜	Night	80 / 82
星星	Stars	82 / 84
星星和螢火蟲	Stars and Fireflies	84 / 86
螢火蟲	Fireflies	86 / 88
夜燈	Nightly Lanterns	88 / 92
山和海	The Sea and the Mountain	92 / 96
山和海	The Sea and the Mountain	96 / 98
海浪	Sea waves	98 / 100
春天	Spring	100 / 102
夏天	Summer	102

秋天 Autumn	104
冬天 Winter	106
秋天 Autumn	108
颱風 A Typhoon	112
下雨 Raining	114
雨 Rain	116
雨 Rain	118
動物園 At a Zoo	120
海天相連 The Sea and the Sky	122
稻草人 A Scarecrow	124
春風 Spring breezes	128
河流 The River	130
木馬 The Wooden Horse	132
蹺蹺板 The Seesaw	134
盪秋千 Playing a Swing	136
天空的花朵 Flowers in the Sky	138
車輛是都市的魚 Vehicles Are Like Fish in the City	140
蝴蝶是會飛的花朵 Butterflies are Flying Flowers	142
房屋是都市的森林 Houses Are the Forest in the City	144
刷牙歌 The Song for Tooth-brushing	148
爸爸媽媽的皺紋 Parents' Wrinkles	150

蠶絲 Silk	152
愛吃糖的螞蟻 Ants that Love Eating Sugar	154
愛生氣的蓮霧 Angry Wax Apples	156
萬能的電話 The Omnipotent Telephone	158
美麗的月亮 The Beautiful Moon	160
愛玩的星星 The Playful Stars	162
愛唱歌的春風 Spring Breezes that Love Singing	164
小氣的白雲 Stingy White Clouds	166
雨給地球洗澡 Rain Is Bathing the Earth	168
山是天空的守護神 The Mountain Is the Guardian Angel of the Sky	170
喜歡抓東西的椰子樹 Palm Trees that Like to Catch Things	172
蜻蜓是一架小飛機 Dragonflies Are Like Airplanes	176
沙白與童詩 Sar Po and His Children's Poetry	180
童詩——人氣之最天真和最美妙的聲音 Children's Poetry Professor Pan Yatun／潘亞暾	186
浪亦難泯的童心：沙白〈海的吼聲〉略讀／余境熹 An Introduction to Tu Shiu-tien (Sar Po)	204
作者簡介 An Introduction to Tu Shiu-tien (Sar Po)	214
陳靖奇教授簡介 Translated by Prof. Ching-chi Chen, Ph.d.	220

沙白的童詩　黃榮村（考試院院長、前中國醫藥大學校長）

沙白是位專業的牙醫師，但更廣為人知的，他是一位長年勤於筆耕，熱心參與國內外核心詩會活動，在國內外都享有名望的詩人。但更特殊的，他也是一般詩人不太敢嘗試的，他一生寫了不少童詩，而且還不是一般應景的童詩。沙白的童詩都很精簡，但它們大部分都包含有詩歌中的重要元素，如比喻、象徵、與想像力。也就是說這是給所有人看的詩歌，其中最關鍵的當然就是，孩童們聽了耳朵都會豎起來，而且一聽再聽。

他走入兒童的世界，跟著他/她們思考跟著感覺走，親近兒童喜歡的事物與具有童趣的題材，譬如說：天空、星星月亮太陽、自然界、風水山海、小動物與動物園、玩具與家具、家人、學校等等。這些題目無一不可入詩，無一不是詩。

假如沙白沒有回歸初心，只是當作詩來寫，則很快會在進出之間被敏感敏銳的小孩抓到，因為他很快看出是為賦童詩而強做幼稚之語而已。所以沙白的高明在此，簡單也在此，因為他很快回歸初心融入場景，唯有在此基礎上，與兒童一起呼吸一起共感，用同樣的語言，都是朋友，若忍不住偶有教化之語，也是自然而然冒出來，孩童也能很快入心。

我們都曾有過童年，大部分的人多以鄉愁與懷念，來回憶觸接自己的童年，只是有點像隔岸相望，中間有一段很長的心理距離。我們應該有更好的方式可以回去童年，與現在的小孩成為朋友，一起生活在大家有共同感覺，用同樣話的成長與學習環境。感謝沙白，他為我們這些寫詩的人，做了一個難得的示範。我們不見得回得去，但是至少我們知道這是可能的，因為沙白經常回去。他用豐富多元又簡短的童詩告訴我們，兒童們其實都在那裡等著我們，要我們有空就一起來玩，一起走入有共同感覺的世界。

A Foreword
Sar Po's Children's Poetry

— **Jong-Tsun Huang (黃榮村), former President,
the Examination Yuan, Republic of China;
former Minister of Education, Republic of China;
and former President, the Chinese Medical University at Taichung.**

Sar Po, a well-known dentist and a well-known poet, has been diligently working on the writing of poetry. He has been in good association with other poets in their daily contact and during some important gatherings. Other poets write poetry for the general reading public; yet, in addition to poetry for the general reading public, Sar Po writes children's poetry which is easy to read and is loved by children. In it, he structures his imagination through the eye of children with some rhetoric techniques, such as comparison (metaphor and simile), symbols, etc. His poetry has been enjoyed by adults and children.

In his children's poetry, he leads us, adults and children alike, in the world conceived through the eye of children. In the poetry, objects such as the sky, the sun, the moon, stars, the sea, rivers, and mountains; living things in and out of botanical and / or zoological gardens; toys and furniture; the school and the family, are all his topics.

Let us suppose if Sar Po did not go back to the primordial state of the mind intentionally and wrote his poetry, some sensitive juvenile readers would still be able to locate the existence of the mind in the poetry. The mind is the children's mind. Each and every one of us, adults and children, harbors the children's mind. Sar Po is good at grasping the children's mind in his poetry, so much so that it appeals to adults and children alike. The poetry is enlightening and educating.

Everyone has had his / her childhood and is nostalgic about it. The nostalgia is similar to that of his hometown. There is a long distance between adulthood and childhood; yet, many desire to go back to the latter. There must be a way with which one may go back to it. It seems to me that one may do so in living with children and share with them the nostalgia. I am thankful to Sar Po in giving us the possible way to go back to our childhood, not in the real world but in imagination, in his poetry. Many of his children's poems are concise and full of images conceived through the eye of children. Reading the poems would make it possible for us to be with children and lead us back to our own childhood.

台北市教育局毛連塭局長 序

童詩是兒童心靈自然流露的結晶。

童詩是啟發兒童心靈的最佳鑰匙。

童詩是教育兒童的最佳讀物。

兒童是國家未來的主人翁，教育兒童是大人的天職。大人寫的兒童詩，對兒童詩想的啟迪幫助很大，也可以豐富兒童天真純潔的心靈。

我國是文化大國，自古以來，文學興盛發達，而詩是文學的精華，歷代如金珠玉環的燦爛詩篇，一直滋養著人類的心靈。

童詩乃詩之一環，近年來蓬勃發展。沙白為詩人醫生，醫術精湛，於求學時期即熱愛文學，今於行醫之餘，仍對文學研究和創作不綴，並有傑出之創作，今將其童詩出版，為兒童詩壇綻開鮮麗的奇葩，供給大家欣賞。

毛連塭

前高雄市教育局長
現任台北市教育局長

民國七十五年七月

Foreword

— By Mao Lianwen, Commissioner, Bureau of Education, Taipei City and formerly Commissioner, Bureau of Education, Kaohsiung City.

Children's poetry is a crystallization of a spontaneous overflow of the children's emotions.

Children's poetry is the best key to open up the mystery of children's mind.

Children's poetry is the best text for children to read in the education of them.

Children are the future of our nation. To educate them is the duty of us the adults.

The adults write poems for children and, through them, we may enlighten their mind and enrich their innocent imagination.

Our nation is one of rich culture. Since ancient times, the production of literature has been abundant. Poetry is the essence of literature. Verses and poems, which are like gold pearls and jade bracelets brilliant to the eye, nourish the mind of the humankind.

Children's poetry has been flourishing in recent years. Sar Po, a poet and dentist, is excellent in his dentistry and in his love for literature. He was enamored of literature in his younger days. As a practicing dentist, he is still interested in doing research in and writing literature. The outcome of his writing is here for us. This collection of children's poetry is something awesome for us to enjoy.

苗栗縣政府
Miaoli County Government

涂院長秀田 惠鑒：

　　時序季夏荔月之際，蓮渚風清，梅庭月朗，敬維諸事，百務迪吉，維祝維頌！

　　素仰 院長學養卓越，奉獻醫學揚名國際，長年勤於文學創作，成就頗豐，績效斐然，深為各界仰望與敬重，文壇譽為「國際詩人」，曷勝抃賀！

　　欣悉 院長大作「星星愛童詩」、「星星亮晶晶」、「唱歌的河流」三本兒童詩集，與國立高師大前英文所所長暨文學院院長陳靖奇教授合作翻譯成英文，並編印成華英雙語的雋永詩冊，供為兒童雙語文學之優良讀物。

　　今喜見大作付梓在即，耀昌願以歡喜之情樂以為推薦，讓優良文學創作得以向下扎根，以培育更多的後輩文學人才，啟發無窮無盡的創新。

苗栗縣長 徐耀昌 敬上
民國110年07月23日

耀昌用箋

Dear Dr. Shiu-tien Tu:

At the time of mid-summer, when all kinds of fruit are ripe and flowers are blossoming, I wish you well.

Your reputation as a dentist and an international poet is well known to us. It is also known that you are well learned and have written extensively in prose and poetry.

It is a pleasure for us to find that three collections of your children's poetry, Twinkle, Twinkle, Little Stars, Stars Love Children's Poetry and Singing Rivers, will be published with their Chinese and English texts. The English rendition was done by Ching-chi Chen, Ph.d., Professor Emeritus of English, National Kaohsiung Normal University. I believe that our children will benefit from the reading of them.

Knowing that their publication would be good for education of our students / pupils, I strongly recommend them to our teachers and parents.

With best regards, I am
Sincerely yours,
Yao-chang Hsu (徐耀昌),
Magistrate, Miaoli County, Taiwan,
Republic of China.
July 23, 2021.

大家都曾上牙科診所看過牙醫，年幼時也都有讀過童詩。牙醫和詩人是很少有交集的兩種專業。但沙白（涂秀田牙醫師）卻能一手幫病人植牙，另一隻手執筆寫出生動的童詩，長期專注地耕耘，他在杏壇和「詩領域」，都散發出耀人的光芒。

沙白寫詩很早，就讀高雄醫學院時，就擔任阿米巴詩社的社長，也是心臟詩社、布穀鳥詩社的成員；他的詩集「太陽的流聲」、「星星亮晶晶」和「星星愛童詩」等，都曾被譯為日文、韓文，在外國的詩壇被廣為推介。

沙白的詩作受到肯定，他也多次受邀參加亞洲詩人大會、世界詩人大會，和世界華文兒童文學筆會等。

沙白的三本兒童詩集「星星亮晶晶」、「星星愛童詩」、「唱歌的河流」，其內容均經國立高雄師範大學前英語所所長暨文學院院長陳靖奇教授翻譯成英文，可中英對照閱讀，是兒童雙語文學的優良讀物，特此推薦。

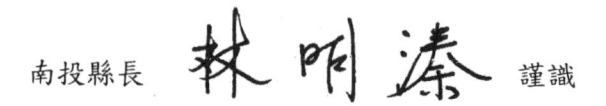

南投縣長　林明溱　謹識

Everybody has visited a dentist and read children's poetry, but dentistry and children's mixed together are rarely seen. Sar Po (Dr. Shiu-tien Tu) can treat his patients' teeth with one hand and write children's poetry with the other. Having written prose and poetry for a long time, he is well known to all.

Sar Po began to write poetry at an early age when he was studying at Kaohsiung Medical University. There he was a member of the following clubs of poetry: The Amoeba Club of Poetry (where he used to serve as its President), The Heart Club of Poetry and The Cuckoo Club of Poetry. Some of his poems in the three collections of his children's poetry, Twinkle, Twinkle, Little Stars, Stars Love Children's Poetry and Singing Rivers, were translated into Japanese and Korean. They are welcome overseas.

He received acclaims from everywhere. He was invited to attend The Asian Congress for Poets, The World Congress for Poets, and the World Congress for Children's Literature in Chinese many times.

The three collections of his children's poetry, Twinkle, Twinkle, Little Stars, Stars Love Children's Poetry and Singing Rivers, will be published with their Chinese and English texts. The English rendition was done by Ching-chi Chen, Ph.d., Professor Emeritus of English, formerly Dean of Liberal Arts, National Kaohsiung Normal University. I believe that our children will benefit from the reading of them.

Knowing that their publication would be good for education of our students / pupils, I strongly recommend them to our teachers and parents.

Mingzhen Lin (林明溱)
Magistrate, Nantou County, Taiwan,
Republic of China.

Penghu County Government

澎湖縣政府

涂院長秀田勛鑒

　　涂院長醫學揚名國際，文學創作豐碩，文壇譽為「國際海洋詩人」。「星星愛童詩」、「星星亮晶晶」、「唱歌的河流」等三本童詩，是我國兒童文學珍貴資產。今與高師大陳靖奇教授合作，將純真雋永的詩篇，編印華、英雙語推廣，令人敬佩。編印之際，謹祝發揚光大，世界看見臺灣兒童文學之美。

　　祝福您與家人平安健康。

澎湖縣 縣長
賴峰偉　　謹上
110 年 5 月 21 日

澎湖縣馬公市治平路32號
32 Chihping RD, Makung Penghu, Taiwan R.O.C
Tel:886-6-9272300 Fax:886-6-9264060

Dear Dr. Shiu-tien Tu,

Your being an expert in dentistry and having written extensively in prose and poetry have helped establish your reputation as a renowned dentist and an international poet. Your three collections of children's poetry, Twinkle, Twinkle, Little Stars, Stars Love Children's Poetry and Singing Rivers, to be published with their Chinese and English texts can be an asset to our education. The English rendition done by Ching-chi Chen, Ph.d., Professor Emeritus of English, National Kaohsiung Normal University, would help the students to enjoy the beauty of poetry and to learn English for their daily life. I believe that our children will benefit from the reading of them in their enjoyment of Taiwan's children's literature and learning of English.

With best regards, I remain
Sincerely yours,
Feng-wui Lai (賴峰偉),
Magistrate, Penghu County, Taiwan,
Republic of China.
May 21, 2021.

邁出了第二步
——談沙白的人和詩

沙白是學醫的，但是他更喜歡文學和孩子。就因為這樣，他跟許多兒童文學工作者成了朋友。沙白寫作勤，除了經常為報紙、雜誌撰稿以外，在文學創作方面寫得多的是新詩。他愛上了兒童文學以後，很自然的也為孩子寫了不少的詩。去年，他把他為孩子寫的詩編成一個集子「星星亮晶晶」，這是他向兒童詩邁出的第一步。今年，他又把一年來為孩子寫的詩編成第二個集子「星星愛童詩」。這是他向兒童詩邁出的第二步。

沙白天性爽朗，再加上意識到他的讀者是小孩子，所以他寫的詩都很明朗。例如他寫的「河流」，就有這樣的特色：

我是一條喜歡旅行的河流

從上游到下游

從山上游到海口

轉了千個彎

唱了萬首歌

日日夜夜流

他既然已經喜歡上了兒童詩，自然會繼續走下去，「深入蠻荒」，尋找屬於他自己的綠洲，他很謙虛，承認他為兒童寫的詩是一種嘗試。其實，那就是他對兒童詩的探索。

林良

16

一個寫兒童詩的人，難免接觸到一些「兒童詩論」。沙白曾經談起：這些詩論大大困擾了他。我想，這是他求好心切的緣故。

詩論的作者，在詩論裏表達了他對「詩」的意見。閱讀詩論可以增長我們對「詩」的見識。詩論的多樣化，提高了「詩論領域」的價值。詩論的可讀，就在詩論作者的各說各話。就因為詩論作者的各說各話，才能對我們的創作產生一些刺激作用。如果天下的詩論竟出現空前的一致，甚至出現了範本，那麼一切創作就都將停工。

我們的小學裏，因為有「童詩教學」活動，在教學過程上不能沒有一定的「秩序」，所以無法避免採用比較科學的態度來處理童詩。童詩必須有「定義」，包括它的性質、形式、內容。一首詩的是不是童詩，要有嚴格的規定。一首詩的好壞，要有明確的立即判斷的標準。以這樣的立場寫出來的詩論，對創作者來說，讀起來當然更是「怕怕」。

購買的先決條件是必須有我們所要的貨品。如果沒有，就只好先放下購買意願，鼓勵製造。我們的童詩世界，目前最需要的是對創作的鼓勵，而不是對創作的「管理」。創作要有良好的環境。

良好的環境不是指一間安靜的房間，而是指一種期待的氣氛。期待的氣氛是：一個人寫了一千首詩，其中只要有一首是你所喜愛的，就立刻介紹給廣大的讀者欣賞。期待要有恒不變，對作者要愛護。慢慢的，我們也就能有好詩「三百首」了。

期待的氣氛不是：一個人剛開始寫了第一首詩，令你失望，就兇狠狠的把他罵回去。

純淨可愛的詩論,其實也並不困擾人;不但不困擾作者有幫助。沙白讀得較多而感到困擾的是可怕的「詩罵」,不但不困擾人,反而對創作者有幫助的人,換一種稿紙,靜下心來依自己的主張多從事創作,多為孩子寫幾首可讀的好詩。

以我國現在兒童詩的總成績來說,自己多種些好花。而且越種越多,總比罵別人小園裏種的都是野草,扛著鋤頭到處巡視,到處剷除好得多。詩的大地是無比的廣濶。

我對沙白說:好詩是歲月和智慧的結晶。對詩,既要朝朝暮暮,也要天長地久。希望我們彼此對對方都有一份期待。你的勤於探索,使我相信你會比我更早找到你自己的綠洲。

（序文作者為中華民國兒童文學會理事長）

七十六年九月五日在台北

Marching out the Second Step:
a Discussion of Sar Po, the Man and His Poetry

—— **Foreword by Lin Liang**

Sar Po majored in dentistry, yet he is also interested in children and literature. That is why he has made friends with people working in the field of literature. He has produced a lot of works and had them published in newspapers and magazines. Among the works, poetry, both new and children's, constitutes the majority. Loving children, he wrote poetry for them. The first collection of children's poetry is entitled, Twinkle, Twinkle, Little Stars. Now, the second collection, Stars Love Children's Poetry, is here with us. That is why I call it marching out the second step.

Sar Po is an open-minded person and, knowing that he is writing poetry for children, his poetry is easy to read. He describes the river as follows:

I am a river who likes to travel,
From up-streams to down-streams, and
From the mountains to the sea.
I make hundreds upon hundreds of turns and
Sing thousands upon thousands of songs,
Day and night.

I believe that, loving children's poetry, he would continue to write more. Marching into the wilds, he would find his oasis. He is humble in saying that writing children's poetry is only a new try. In truth, he is exploring a terra incognito.

To write children's poetry, he has read some poetics on it. Oftentimes, he said that poetics on children's poetry had puzzled him. I believe that the puzzlement is a sign of his desiring to write better poetry.

It seems to me that a writer on his own poetics has his own view of poetry writing. Reading poetics on children's poetry would of course enhance our view on it, but different theories on its writing could sometimes be conflicting. Indeed, different views could offer us different ideas on children's poetry. If all views are the same and unified, there would be no need to write more poetry.

In our primary schools, we have the course, Reading of Children's Poetry. There should be a definitive form of the course. We could not avoid applying some scientific approaches toward the teaching. In the teaching of children's poetry, the elements of the course are as follows: its nature, its form and its content. Whether or not a poem is a children's poem, there is a strict definition. Regrettably, poetry that meets the above-mentioned qualities would be something unwelcome to the writers.

In shopping for goods, we purchase the ones that satisfy our demand. If there is none in the market, we may turn to the production of new goods that satisfy our needs. In the same manner, we may write children's poetry that can satisfy our needs in the classroom. At present, what we need should be encouragement to write good children's poetry, not trying to administer its writing according to the rules set by any authority. In short, what we need is a good environment where poetry can be produced.

A good environment is not one that just offers a quiet space, but an atmosphere where we may anticipate something good and suitable for the writing of poetry. In an atmosphere where such anticipation occurs, the poet may compose a thousand pieces of poetry, only one of which may be to the liking of the readers. This only one can be publicized and introduced to the general public. Feeling of anticipation should be there, and the poet should be encouraged. Little by little, poems produced can amount to as many as Three Hundred Poems of the Tang Dynasty.

In an atmosphere where anticipation occurs, a disappointing poem might be produced. We might negatively criticize its inadequacy according to rules we have set.

Frankly speaking, an acceptable poetics is not that horrible and puzzling. It might help the poet along in his writing. I know that many negatively criticize some of the poems by Sar Po. I wish that those who criticize would leave him alone and try to write poems themselves for the good of the children.

It seems to me that in the garden of children's poetry, we should plant more flowers. We should not claim that flowers planted by others might be weeds. We should not carry hoes everywhere trying to destroy flowers planted by others as weeds. The more flowers there are, the better. The Good Earth is immense and is able to contain all.

I would like to say to Sar Po that good poetry is a crystallization of time and wisdom. Poetry is about temporariness and eternity. We should hope him well. We believe that, ceaselessly exploring in the realm of poetry, he would find his oasis.

By Lin Liang, President of the Association of Children's Literature, Republic of China, September 1987.

自序

一九九〇年五月我參加中國大陸湖南舉行的「世界華文兒童文學筆會」，我發表了論文「兒童詩的探索」（刊於民國79年5月31日國語日報」。內容概述如下：「一、兒童詩的內涵：兒童詩是人類童真、童趣、童善、童美的表現。童真：兒童的心靈最真實純樸、不虛偽，由『裸體的國王』故事，可見一斑。意趣、趣味是兒童文學的重要成份，……童趣可以說是兒童文學的第一要素。童善：善就是好，即對自己、對他人和對社會都有益的好。具有童善的兒童詩，即具有詩之啟發性、教育性和社會性。童美：愛美是人類的天性。……童美和童趣可以引起兒童的閱讀興趣，在無形中，能夠陶冶性情、發揮其天然的童真，並達成兒童善的效果。也就是在感覺上和知覺上，對事物之詩感及其意象之表現，容易為兒童感應的詩。……三、兒童詩的效用；兒童文學（尤其是兒童詩）不是小小文學，不止是屬於兒童的東西，也是人類最原始、最基本、最純潔的靈魂的故鄉和聖地，是最值得尊重的文學。……總之，兒童詩是人類中，最珍貴的文藝品。」

兒童詩如此珍貴、神聖，因此，我雖然寫了許多成人詩和散文，也已經出版了兩本童詩集「星星亮晶晶」和「星星愛童詩」，我還是繼續寫着兒童詩，像一條永遠唱歌不停的河流，像日月運行不止，與百川奔流並進。

我的兒童詩曾經被譯為日文、韓文，為外國的孩童們喜讀，也在中國大陸許多報紙和雜誌介紹過，大陸的兒童也很喜歡，可見世界上許多孩童的心靈都是相同的。

大陸名作家阿紅於「沙白與童詩」中說：「沙白的兒童詩富有兒童趣味、兒童想像；重視智育、德育、美育，內容寬闊；使用有節奏感的口語，比較自由。我念一些給冬冬南南聽，孩子聽得小眼烏亮。……孩子聽了詩，爭着要書。」

廣州暨南大學教授潘亞暾，於「童詩—人籟之最天真和最美妙的聲音」中說：「沙白的童詩集我曾給很多學齡前兒童和小學低年級學生看過，他們都愛不釋手，在沙白創造的神奇的童詩世界中一個個流連忘返，迫使我看到‥善良、純潔是兒童的天性，台灣、大陸乃至普天之下都一樣。沙白的詩是怎麼牽動孩子們心的?我深感沙白確是一位洞察兒童心靈的詩人。他的童詩既富於兒童情趣,又蘊含着豐富的內容,幫助小讀者開闊眼界,拓展思路,領悟生活道理,形象思維和邏輯思維結合得很好,熔教育性、知識性、藝術性於一爐,實爲童詩中的上品,在詩的構思、描寫、思想的提煉、形象的塑造和語言運用諸方面,都有獨到之處。」

前中華民國兒童文學學會理事長林良説:「我對沙白説:好詩是歲月和智慧的結晶。對詩,既要朝朝暮暮,也要天長地久。」

這本詩集「唱歌的河流」,是繼「星星亮晶晶」和「星星愛童詩」後的第三本兒童詩集,不但給兒童詩的天空增添了一顆明亮有趣的星星,也在兒童文學的天地,多譜了一些美妙的童詩歌聲,希望能夠引起大家更多的欣賞樂趣。

24

Preface

In May 1990, I attended a Conference for World Children's Literature in Chinese sponsored by the Poets, Editors and Novelists (PEN) Association in Hunan, China Mainland. There, I read a paper entitled "Exploring Children's Poetry," which was published in the Guoyu Newspaper, May 31, 1990. The content of the paper is as follows: "One, the purpose of children's poetry is to express children's innocence, interest, virtue and beauty. Children's poetry is man's detergent, lubricant and nutrient. Children's mind, not being hypocritical, is the truest and the purest. This can be shown in the fable of "The King's Clothes." Interest and taste are important elements in children's poetry. Children's interest is the first element in their literature. Children's virtue is the good children possess toward themselves, others and society. Poetry with children's virtue can be enlightening, educative and socializing to children. The beauty and interest in children's poetry can invite children to read it. Their reading would imperceptibly mold their character and help foster their innocence. Two, I would like to define children's poetry as one that contains spirit of children and consciousness of children. The things described in the poetry can be perceptually and intelligently accepted and enjoyed by children. Three, the effect of children's poetry can be as follows: Children's literature, especially children's poetry, is not little literature. It belongs not only to children. Things discussed in it are the homeland and the holy land of man's most primordial, most fundamental, and purest mind and spirit. Truly, children's poetry is the most precious art form of the humankind.

As stated above, children's poetry is precious and holy. I have written prose and poetry for the general public. Recently, two collections of my children's poetry, Twinkle, Twinkle, Little Stars and The Stars Love Children's Poetry, have been published. I would like to continue to write like a river ceaselessly singing, time moving continuously and all rivers and streams rushing to the sea endlessly.

My poems have been translated into Korean and Japanese. Apparently, they are well received by children overseas. They are likewise well received by those on Mainland China, according to some local newspapers. It is clear that children everywhere share the same mind and joy of reading of children's poetry.

A Mainland Chinese writer, A-hong, says in his essay, "Sar Po and His Children's Poetry," Sar Po's poetry is rich in children's interest and imagination. Through it, children's education of intelligence, of virtue and of aesthetics can be carried on. His poetry is in rhythmic everyday speeches. It is in the form of free verse. I read some poems to children and they were surprised and wanted to read more from the collections of Sar Po's children's poetry."

Professor Pan Yatun, of Jinan University, Guangzhou, in "Children's Poetry is the Most Innocent and the Most Melodious Voice" comments, "I asked many primary-school students to read Sar Po's poetry so much that they would not put it down. In the wonderful world created in the poetry, we see virtue and innocence of children there. I think that everywhere children are the same. How can the poetry touch them? The answer should be: Sar Po is one who is able to see the secrecy of children's mind. His poetry is one of children's interest and of rich imagination in helping the students to open their eyes to their own world, to explore their potentialities of thinking and enlighten them to some fundamentals of life. In the poetry, the combination of thinking in images and logic is well integrated. In it, education, knowledge and arts are well melted in one furnace. His poetry is the best. In short, the structuring of poetic images, the description of them, the refinement of ideas, and the employment of language have hit home to the core of excellence."

Lin Liang, former President of the Republic of China Children's Literature Association, said, "I told Sar Po that good poetry is a crystallization of time and intelligence. Good poetry would be of everyday life and would exist everlastingly."

The present collection, The Singing Rivers, is the third after Twinkle, Twinkle, Little Stars and The Stars Love Children's Poetry. I wish that the third one would add another bright star in the sky of children's poetry and that there would be one more melodious voice there. I wish that my poetry would furthermore entertain you in your reading and chanting.

唱歌的河流

河流是流浪的歌手
從山上流到海口
一面旅行一面唱歌
她是快樂的歌手

——兒童的雜誌 77年9月10日

A Singing River

The river is a wandering singer.
The river flows from the high mountains to the sea.
She sings all the way.
She is a happy singer.

—Children's Magazine, September 10, 1988.

石頭

那麼多卵石躺在河邊
好像是漲水時河流生下的蛋
卻永遠躺在那裡
孵不出可愛的小雞

—民生報 79年3月3日

Pebbles

There are so many pebbles on the river bank.
They are like eggs laid by the rising water of the sea.
They will lie there eternally and
Little chickens would not come out of them.

—The Minsheng Newspaper, March 3, 1990.

春天

眼睛看不完的春天
耳朵聽不完的春天
雙手抓不完的春天
我們有很多春天

花開鳥叫
使春天熱鬧
而母親的微笑
是最美麗的春天

——國語日報 76年4月4日

Springtime

We got many springs, and
We can never grab all springs.
Our ears can never hear all springs.
Our eyes can never see all springs.

Flowers bloom and birds chirp,
Making springs lively.
To me, my mother's smile
Seems to be the most beautiful spring

—Guoyu Newspaper, April 4, 1987.

苦和樂

果樹吃了鹹鹹的肥料以後，會長出甜甜的果實；生病吃了苦藥以後，會恢復健康的身體；功課認真苦讀以後，會有得滿分的樂趣。

——國語日報78年12月12日

Bitterness and Sweetness

Having absorbed salty fertilizer,
Fruit trees would yield sweet fruit.
A patient who has taken bitter medicine
Would recover from his illness and be healthy again.
Having studied hard,
A student would enjoy the pleasure of gaining a full score.

—Guoyu Newspaper, December 12, 1989.

球

你沒有腳卻能跳得那麼高
你沒有翅膀卻能飛得那麼遠
原來你會變魔術
把翅膀和腳
隱藏在圓圓的肚子裏
讓我們看了傻笑

——國語日報 77年5月24日

A Ball

You have no feet, and yet you can jump so high.
You have no wings, and yet you can fly to faraway places.
You are a magician,
Being able to hide your feet and wings
In your round belly.
Knowing this, I am forced to giggle.

—Taiwan Times, March 24, 1988.

母雞

母雞帶小雞
教他們一起吃
母雞捨不得吃
讓小雞先吃
都是慈母意
孩兒知不知？

——台灣時報 77年3月26日

The Hen

The hen leads little chickens
And teaches them to pick up food to eat.
The hen is saving food for the little chickens to eat.
The chickens eat first.
The hen is like a loving mother.
As children, do we really know the kindness of
   our loving mothers?

    —Taiwan Times, March 26, 1988.

小狗

小狗汪汪叫
原來叫小貓
小貓妙妙叫
一起湊熱鬧
弟弟妹妹一起吵
都被狠狠的竹棍趕跑

——台灣時報 78年2月16日

Puppies

Little puppies bark,
Calling little kittens.
The little kittens meow.
The little puppies and the little kittens
    are noisy together.
In the same manner, brothers and sisters are noisy,
And are scared away by the mother's rod.

    —Taiwan Times, February 16, 1989.

小公雞

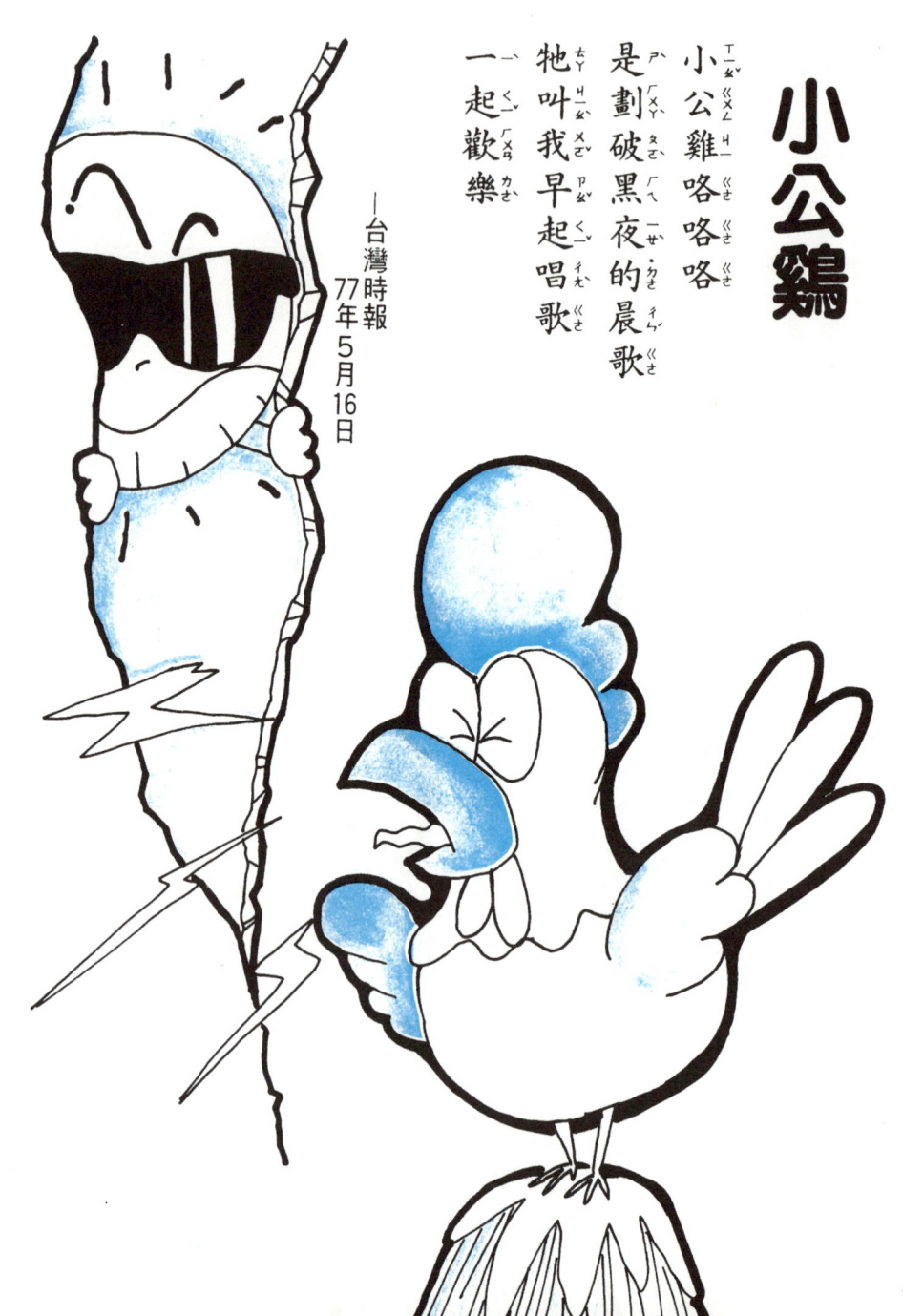

小公雞咯咯咯
是劃破黑夜的晨歌
牠叫我早起唱歌
一起歡樂

—台灣時報 77年5月16日

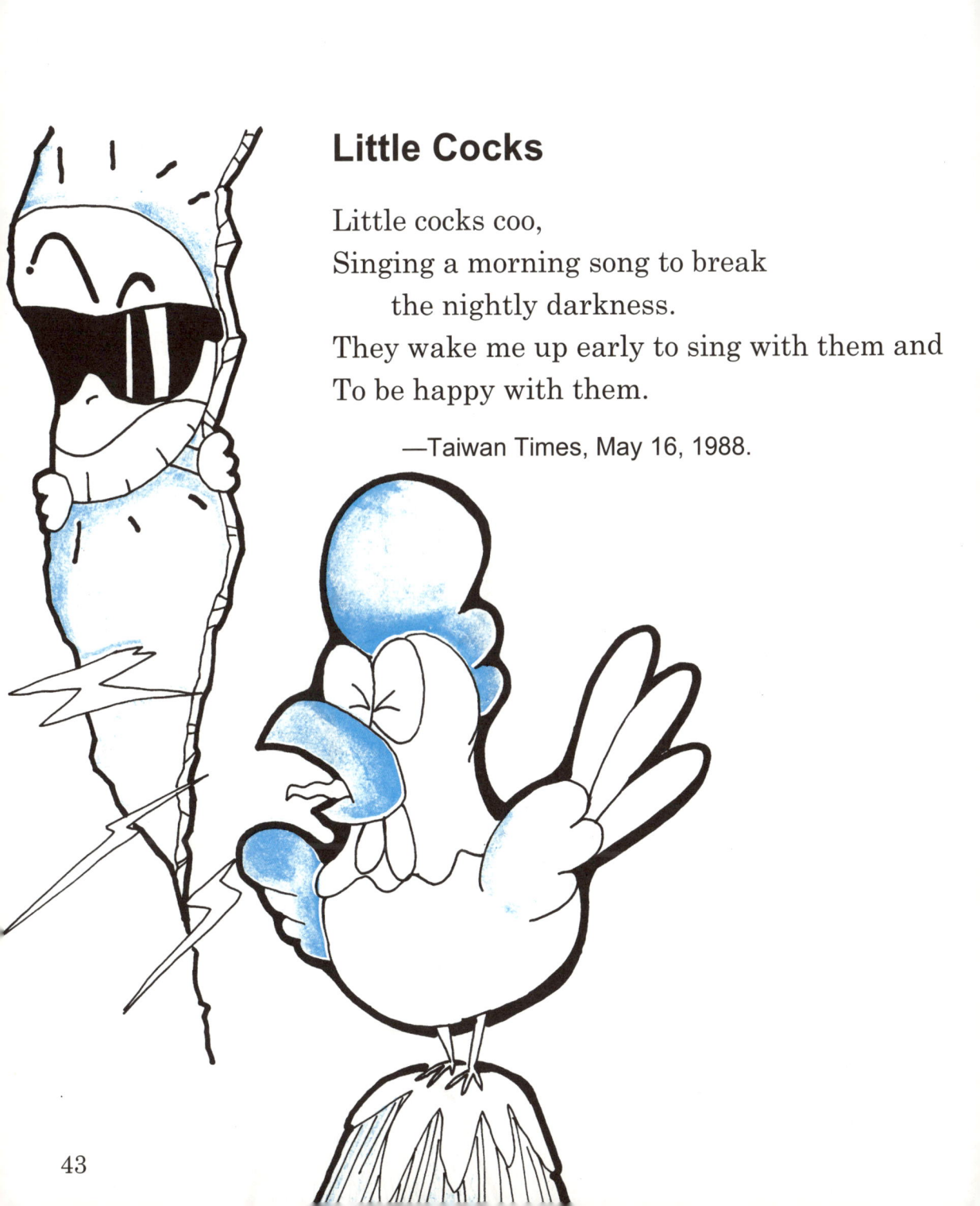

Little Cocks

Little cocks coo,
Singing a morning song to break
    the nightly darkness.
They wake me up early to sing with them and
To be happy with them.

—Taiwan Times, May 16, 1988.

猪

肥肥的猪胖嘟嘟
肥肥的猪吃飽肚
肥肥的猪睡呼呼
不知何時被抓走
殺了給人煮

——台灣時報 78年2月4日

Piggies

How plump the piggies are !
They eat all day.
They sleep all day.
They do not know
When they will be taken away and
Slaughtered and cooked.

—Taiwan Times, February 4, 1989.

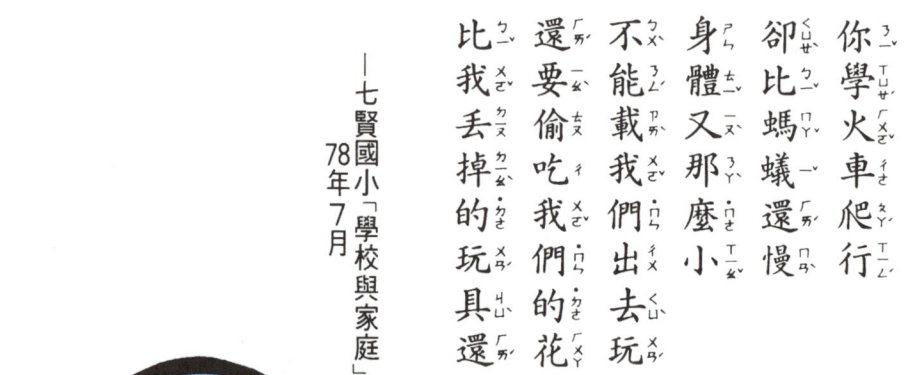

毛毛蟲

你學火車爬行
卻比螞蟻還慢
身體又那麼小
不能載我們出去玩
還要偷吃我們的花木和嫩草
比我丟掉的玩具還糟糕

—七賢國小「學校與家庭」
78年7月

A Caterpillar

You are learning to run like a train, and yet
You crawl more slowly than ants.
Your body is so small
That you cannot carry us around to play.
Instead, you stealthily eat away our flowers
    and twigs and green grass.
You are worse than my discarded toys.

    — School and Family Journal,
      Qishian Primary School, July 1989.

園物植

—台灣時報 77年11月22日

繁花綠葉開滿園
荷花池塘在中間
洗了清新森林浴
快快樂樂過一年

48

The Botanical Garden

Flowers and green leaves can be found in the garden, and
A lotus pond is in the middle of it.
Being there, I, having taken a forest bath, feel
Refreshed and happy at the time of New Year.

—Taiwan Times, November 22, 1988.

腳踏車

腳踏車是最乖的馬
它只有兩隻腳
不會亂跑
它不喝水、不吃草
不隨便尿尿
是最可愛的鐵馬

——七賢國小「學校與家庭」
78年7月

The Bicycle

The bicycle is a tame horse;
Yet it has only two feet.
It will never run about at will.
It neither drinks water nor eats grass.
It never pees.
It is a lovely steel horse.

— School and Family Journal, Qishian Primary School, July 1989.

大冬瓜

你實在太胖了
軟弱的莖撐不起你圓胖的身體
你必須躺在地上
吸水生活

人太胖了
小小的腳也撐不住巨大的身體
容易病倒
躺在床上
靠打點滴維持生命

——「高市兒童」第九期
79年7月

The Big Winter Melon

You are so plump and huge that
The little stem cannot hold you up.
You have to lie down to suck water
And grow.
In the same manner, an overly obese person
Cannot be held up by weak slim feet.
Lying down in bed,
It is easy for him to get sick and
He has to stay alive through dripping of nutrients
   at a hospital.

    —Kaohsiung Children's Journal, #9,
      July 1990.

蠟燭

你一點火
就開始工作
滴著熱騰騰的血汗
那是你熱誠工作的結晶
燃燒自己
照亮別人的標誌

——兒童文學 78年5月

The Candle

Once lighted,
You begin to work.
You sweat warm blood to show that
You work fervently.
The blood is a crystallization proving
 that you love your work.
That you burn yourself
Is a sign of your shining a bright way
 for others.

—Children's Literature, May 1989.

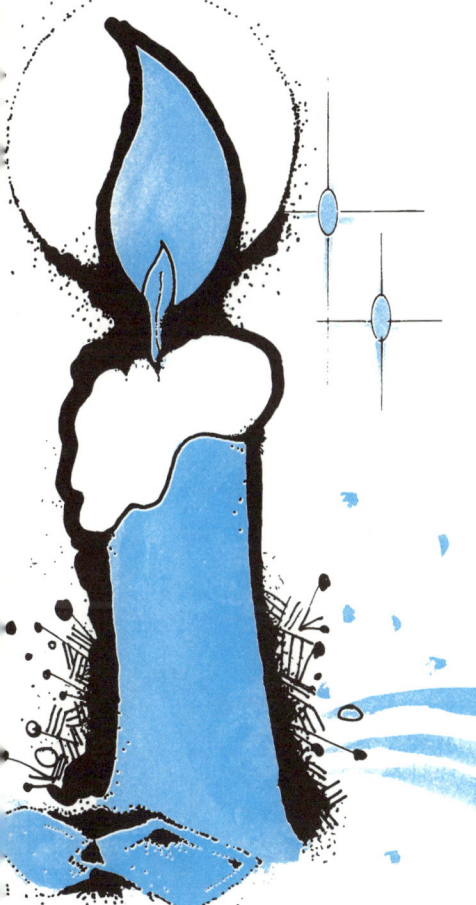

鏡子

我對你笑嘻嘻
你也對我笑嘻嘻
我哭哭涕涕
你也哭哭涕涕
你是我最好的朋友
也是我的雙生兄弟

——七賢國小「學校與家庭」78年7月

The Mirror

I smile at you, and
You also smile at me.
I cry in tears, and
You also cry in tears.
You are my best friend, and
You are also my twin brother.

— School and Family Journal, Qishian Primary School, July 1989.

小鳥的歌聲

小鳥唱出美妙的歌聲
美妙的歌聲也有翅膀
飛入我們的耳朵
在耳朵裡遨翔
感動我們的心房
一起歡樂
一起歌唱

──美國世界日報 79年6月13日

The Chirping of Little Birds

Little birds sing beautiful songs.
The songs also have wings.
They fly into our ears.
The sweet songs wander in our ears,
Moving us to be happy and
Inviting us to sing with them.

    —American World Newspaper, June 13, 1990,

鳥的快樂

—七賢國小「學校與家庭」
78年7月

鳥有唱歌的快樂
鳥有飛翔的快樂
卻沒有我們坐飛機那麼快樂

Happy Birds

Happy birds sing, and
Happy birds fly.
But they are not so happy as we are flying in planes.

— School and Family Journal, Qishian Primary School, July 1989.

美麗的世界

美麗的世界
有美麗的花朵
美麗的衣服
美麗的房屋
美麗的玩具
而最美麗的是
小朋友的天真歌聲、笑聲
和純潔感人的詩語

——「高市兒童」第九期
　　79年7月

The Beautiful World

The beautiful world
Has beautiful flowers,
Beautiful clothes,
Beautiful houses and
Beautiful toys.
But the most beautiful are
Children's innocent songs and laughters, and
Their pure, touching poetic language.

—Kaohsiung Children' Journal, #9, July 1990.

夢

夢是會飛的美妙戲劇
它演得很精彩
它怕眼睛看
我的眼睛一張開
就被無形的鳥兒銜走了
一直找不到

——七賢國小「學校與家庭」78年7月

A Dream

A dream is like a sweet drama that flies.
The drama is exciting, and yet
It is afraid of being seen.
As soon as I open my eyes,
It will be bit off by an invisible bird,
Nowhere to be found.

   —School and Family Journal,
    Qishian Primary School, July 1989.

月餅

―兒童文學 78年5月

月餅是地球上不會發光的月亮
一到中秋節就擺滿街上
許多地球上的月亮被吃掉了
只有天上光明的月亮沒被吃掉
否則明年中秋節就沒月亮可看

Mooncakes

On earth, mooncakes are moons that do not glow.
At Mid-autumn Festival, they are everywhere
    to be found in the market.
Many of the earthly moons are eaten.
I wish that the one in the sky would not be eaten;
Otherwise, there would be no moon for
    us to see next Mid-autumn Festival.

    —Children's Literature, May 1989.

我是一隻蠟燭

我是一隻蠟燭
給大家希望
給大家溫暖
要燃燒熊熊的火光
我是一隻蠟燭
要燃燒熊熊的火光
驅除邪惡
招來善良

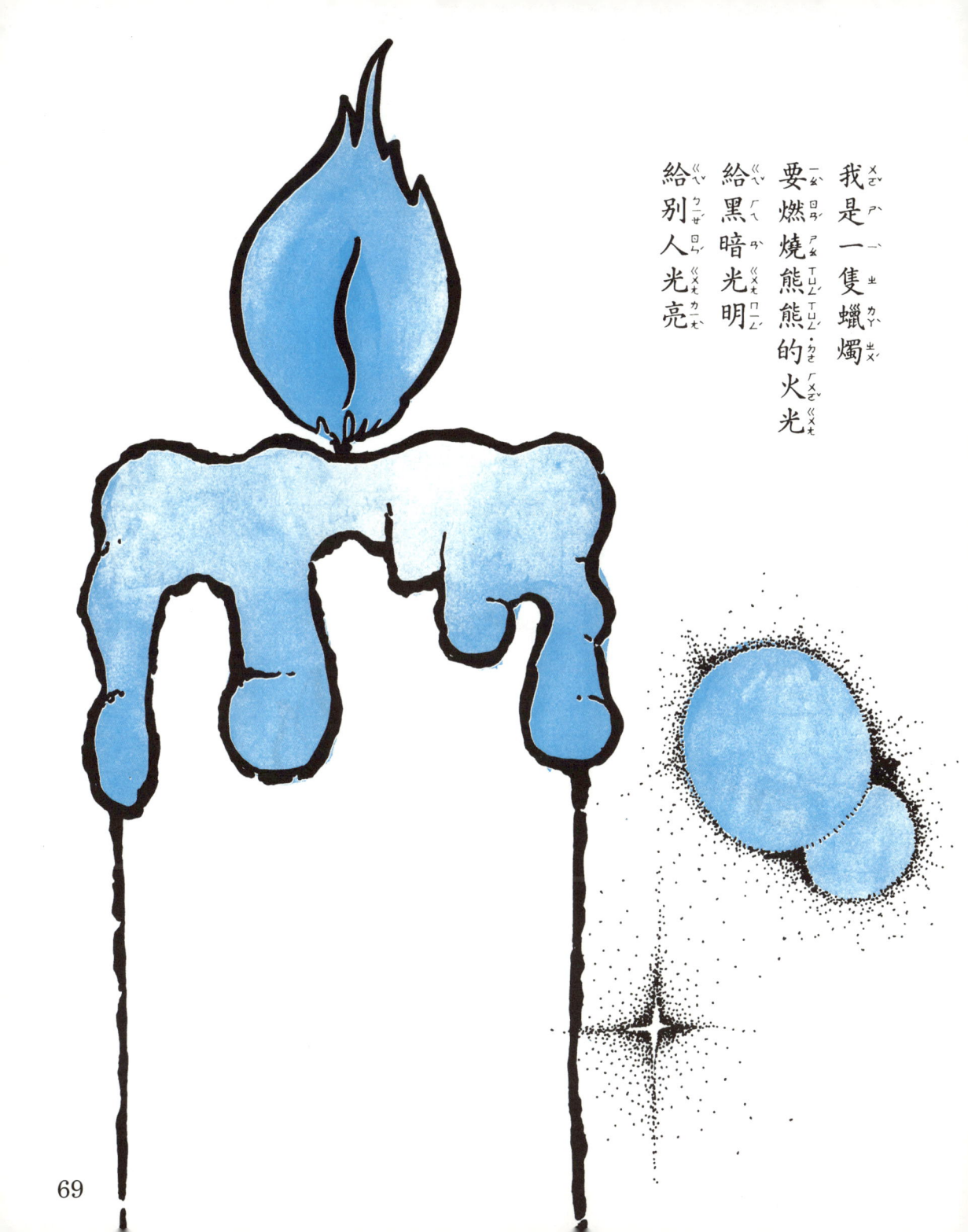

我是一隻蠟燭
要燃燒熊熊的火光
給黑暗光明
給別人光亮

If I were a Candle

If I were a candle,
I would burn myself in great fire
To give warmth to everybody and
To bring everybody hope.

If I were a candle,
I would burn myself in great fire
To drive away evil and
To bring kindness.

If I were a candle,
I would burn myself in great fire
To get rid of darkness and
To light up for others.

一朵美麗的花

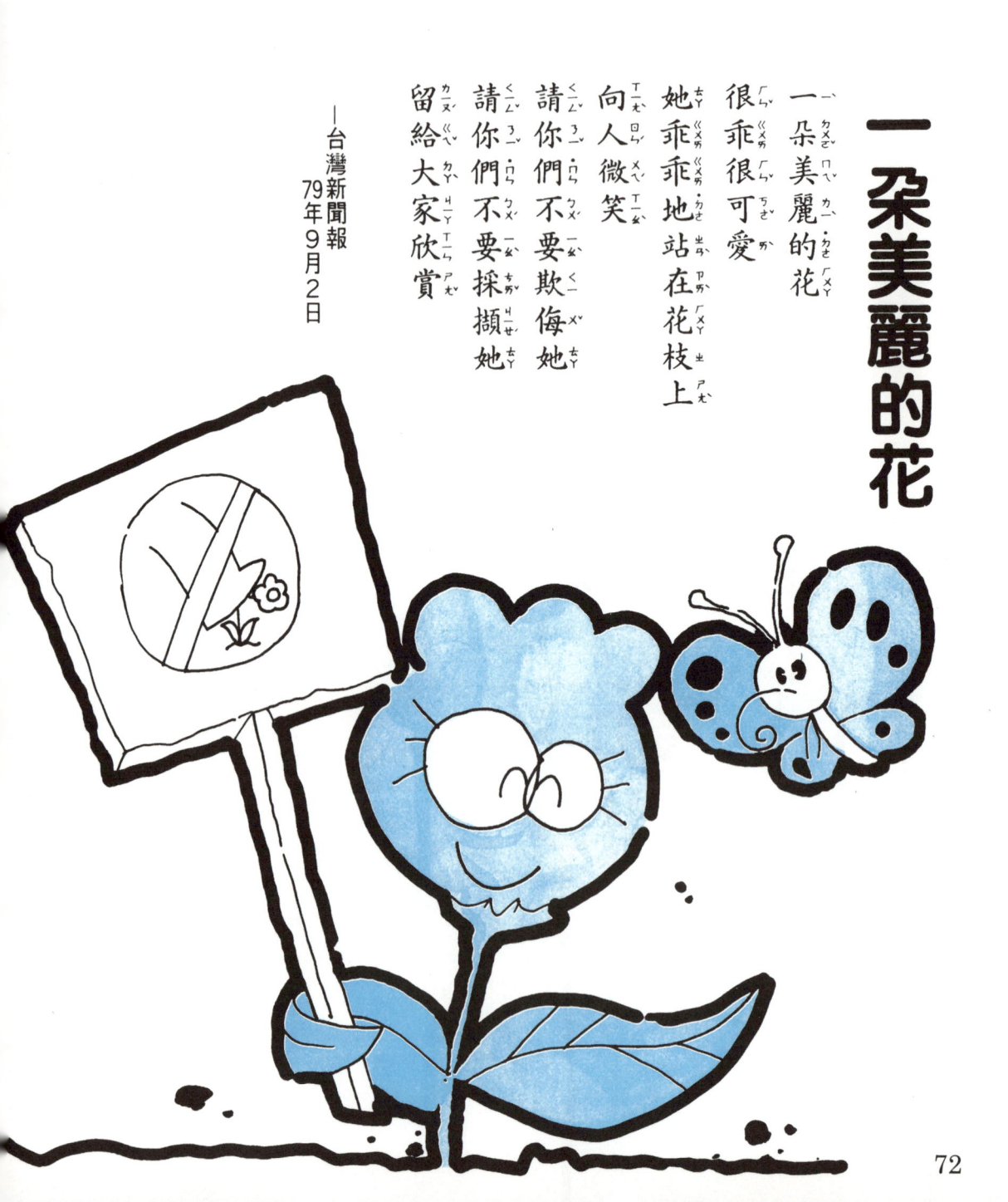

一朵美麗的花
很乖很可愛
她乖乖地站在花枝上
向人微笑
請你們不要欺侮她
請你們不要採擷她
留給大家欣賞

—台灣新聞報
79年9月2日

A Beautiful Flower

A beautiful flower,
Quietly and lovably,
Grows on a twig of a tree.
She is smiling at passers-by.
Please don't bully her.
Please don't destroy her.
She is there for everyone to enjoy her beauty.

    —Taiwan Times, September 2, 1989

初秋的落葉

一片最有情的樹葉
聞到秋天的氣息
就悲傷起來
不小心從樹上掉落下來
離別了他的父母兄弟姊妹
流浪在泥土上
嗦嗦地哭訴流浪的痛苦

Fallen Leaves in Early Autumn

A sentimental leaf,
Smelling the breath of the coming autumn,
Is sad.
He accidentally falls down from the tree,
Leaving his parents, brothers and sisters.
He wanders everywhere on earth,
Tremblingly crying and telling the pains
    of his wandering life.

時間

時間是一隻永不回頭的小鳥
日日夜夜,一直向前飛

然而
牠總是偷偷摸摸地飛
我們要好好地抓住牠
好好地珍惜牠
不要讓牠溜走

Time

Time is like a bird that never returns.
It flies onward day and night.

In truth,
It flies away stealthily.
We have to grab it and
              Cherish it.
We have to hold it firmly in our hands.

日夜

白天　太陽演戲
晚上　月亮和星星演戲
白天的戲熱烘烘
晚上的戲冷清清
所以太陽公公賺了最多錢
不怕繳巨額的電燈費
白天就很亮
而月亮和星星賺的錢很少
所以要節省用電
晚上就很暗

—台灣時報 77年6月6日

Day and Night

In the daytime, the sun plays his part;
At night, the moon and the stars play theirs.
In the daytime, the drama is hot and boisterous.
At night, it seems to be deserted.
Grandpa Sun earns a lot of money from his audience;
He is not afraid to pay a high electricity bill.
That is why, during the daytime, there is light everywhere.
On the contrary, the moon and the stars earn far less;
They have to save electricity carefully, and
There is darkness everywhere at night.

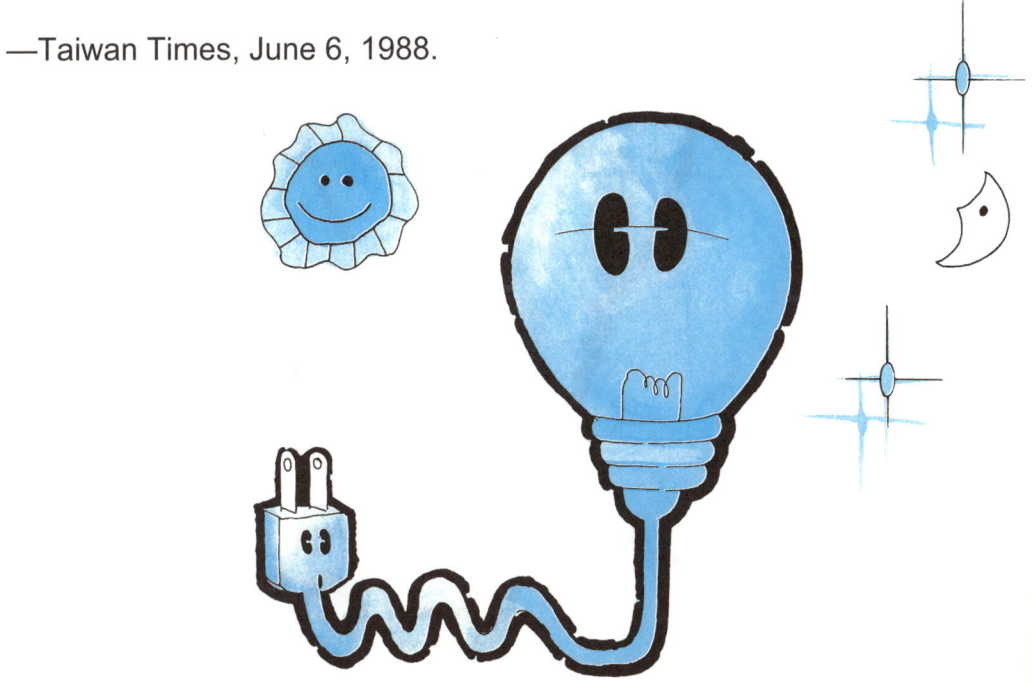

—Taiwan Times, June 6, 1988.

夜

夜好厲害
用一塊巨大的黑布
嚇走了太陽公公
原來她要
命令他下山
請月亮姊姊和星星妹妹們出來
表演精彩的夜戲給我們看

——台灣時報 77年6月10日

Night

Night is amazing.
She uses a gigantic black cloth
To scare away Grandpa Sun and
To order him to go down the mountains.
Oh, I got it.
She wants Sister Moon and Sisters Stars to come out
To play a nightly drama for us to watch.

—Taiwan Times, June 10, 1988.

星星

天上有無數的星星
星星是黑夜的眼睛
天空太大
要由許多星星來照顧

—兒童文學 78年5月

Stars

There are countless stars.
The stars are the eyes of the black night.
The sky, which is huge,
Needs a lot of stars to take care of it.

—Children's Literature, May 1989.

星星和螢火蟲

星星一閃一閃亮晶晶
螢火蟲一閃一閃比美麗
星星在天上發信號
螢火蟲在地上通信息
他們互相交談遊戲
並探求宇宙的秘密
請我們去解謎

―台灣時報 77年6月2日

Stars and Fireflies

Twinkle, twinkle, little stars!
Twinkle, twinkle, little fireflies!
They are vying each other for beauty.
It seems that the stars are sending messages above
    in the sky, and
That the fireflies are sending messages here on earth.
Both seem to be playing a game of communication,
Exploring the secret of the universe.
We are supposed to solve the riddle of it.

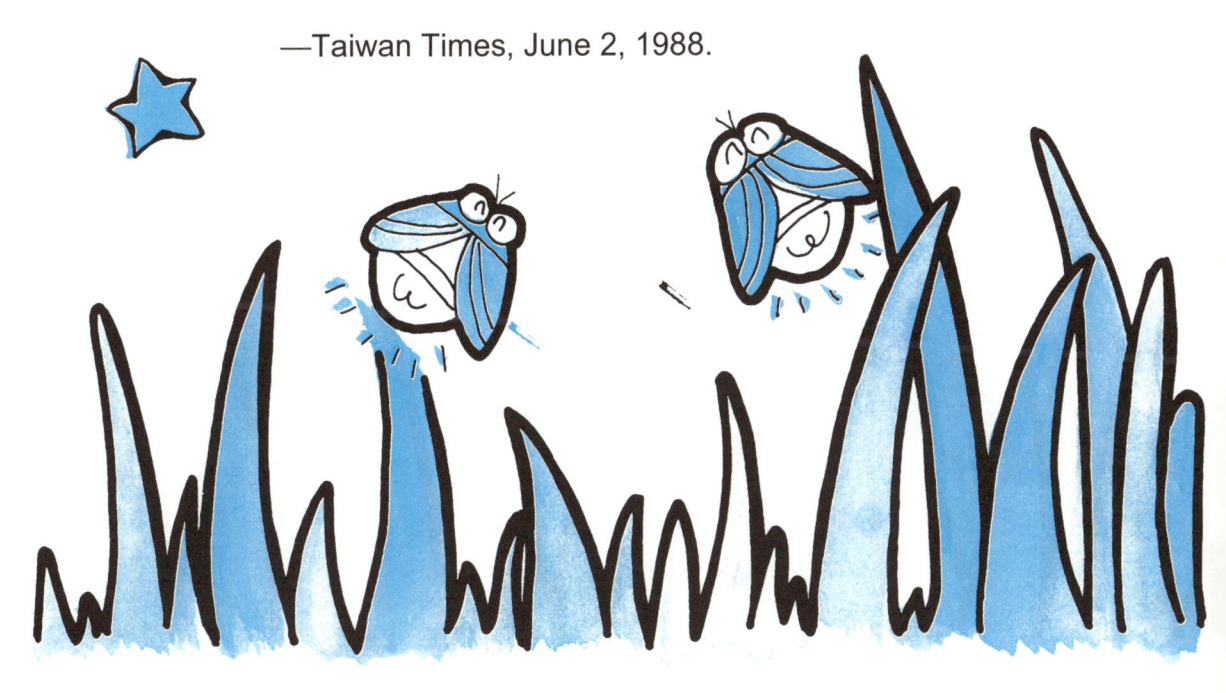

—Taiwan Times, June 2, 1988.

螢火蟲

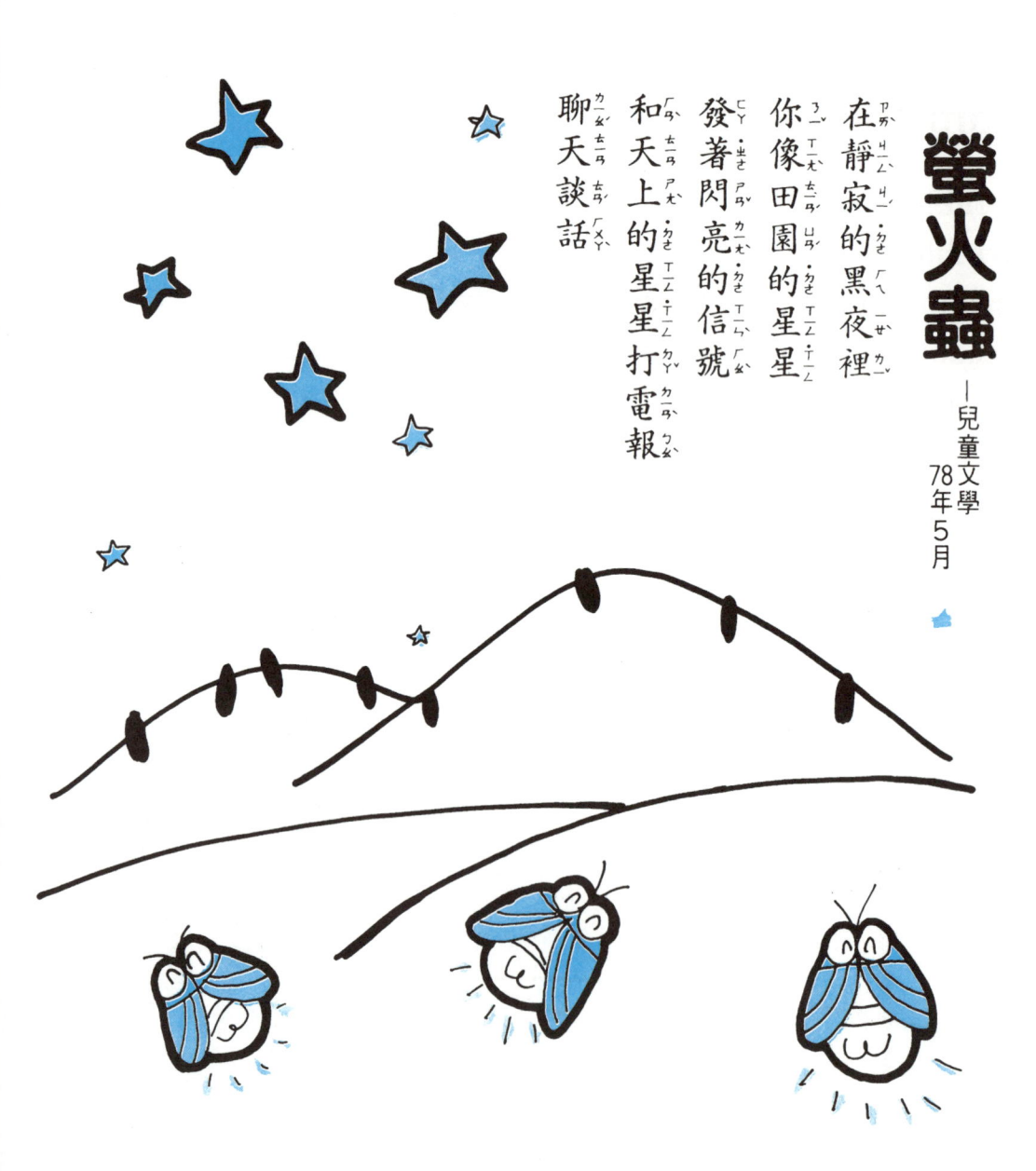

——兒童文學 78年5月

在靜寂的黑夜裡
你像田園的星星
發著閃亮的信號
和天上的星星打電報
聊天談話

Fireflies

In our silent night,
You look like stars in the field,
Giving blinking signals.
You seem to be sending telegram to the stars in the sky
For some idle conversation.

—Children's Literature, May 1989.

夜燈

每個晚上
都有許多星星飛下來
在地上閃閃發光
飛到城市的星星最多最美麗
由山上向城市眺望
白色、紅色、綠色各種大小星星笑嘻嘻
好像一群仙女下凡
給寂寞的地球樂趣

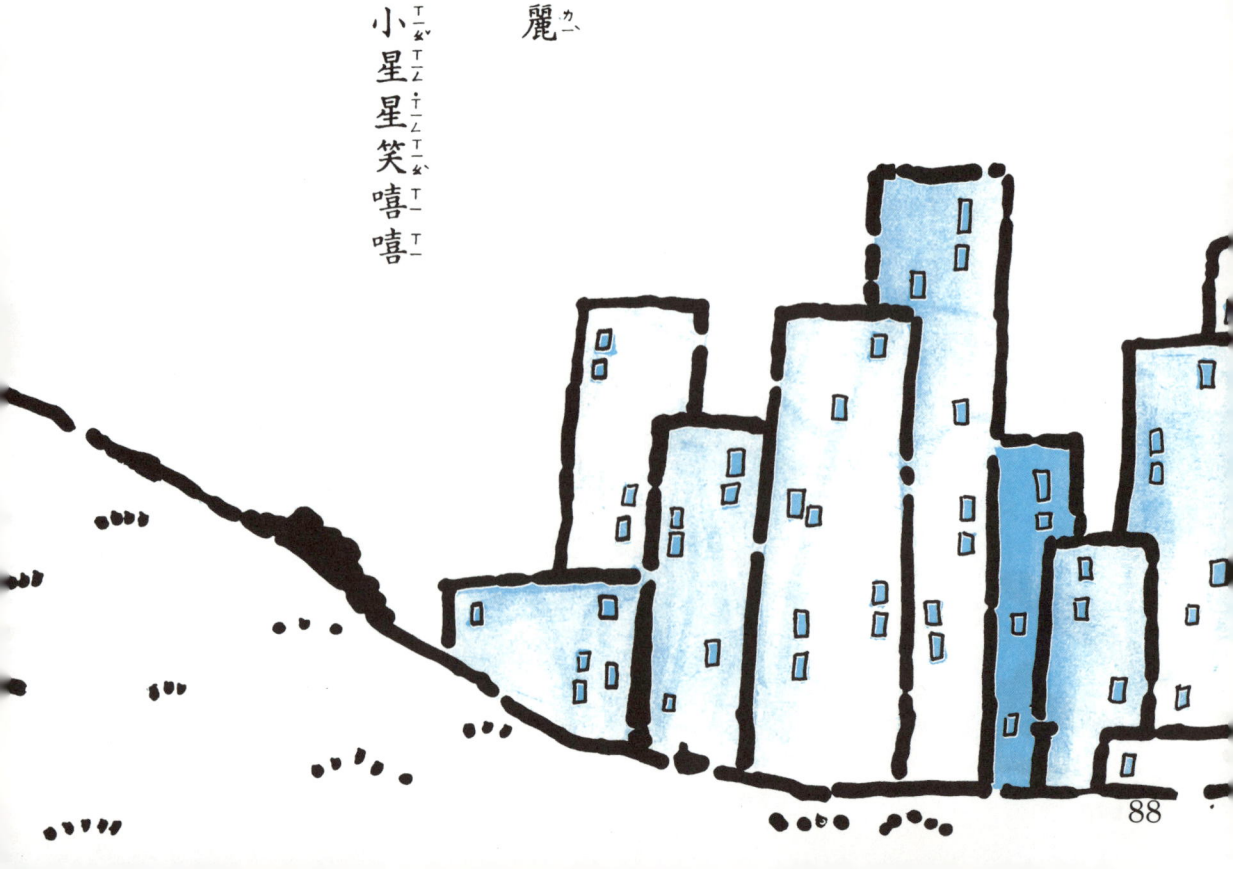

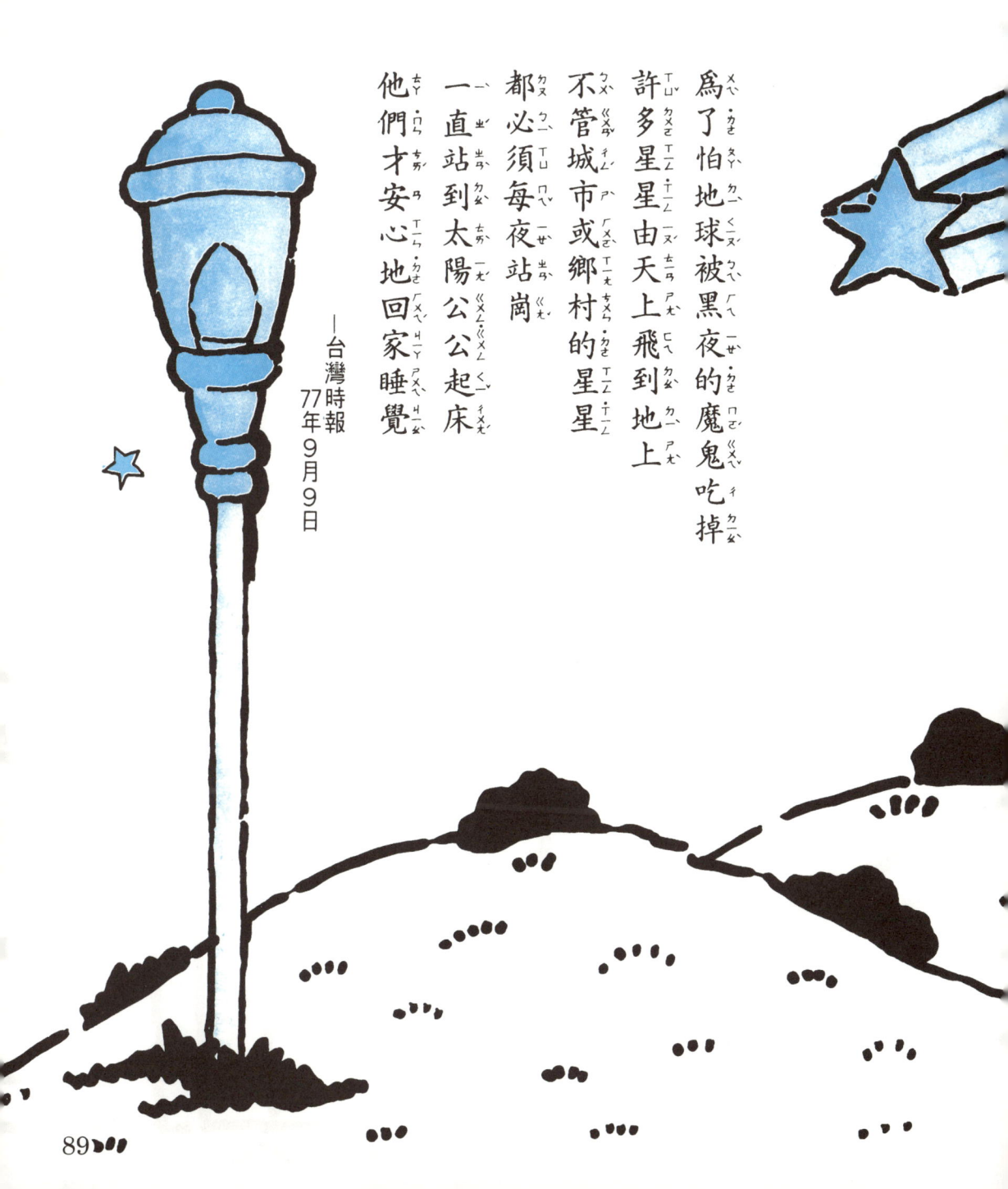

為了怕地球被黑夜的魔鬼吃掉
許多星星由天上飛到地上
不管城市或鄉村的星星
都必須每夜站崗
一直站到太陽公公起床
他們才安心地回家睡覺

——台灣時報 77年9月9日

Nightly Lanterns

Every night,
Many comets seem to have come down from the sky,
Blinking on earth.

Those that fly to big cities are many and they are beautiful.
Overlooking from the top of a mountain,
One can see little stars of white, red and green colors laughing.
They are all like fairies flying to the ground
Giving joy to the earth.

For fear that the earth would be eaten by nightly demons,
Many stars seem to have come down from the sky to guard it.
In cities and in the countryside, there are stars on guard.
They are there all night until Grandpa Sun wakes up.
Not until then would they go home to bed.

—Taiwan Times, September 9, 1988.

山和海

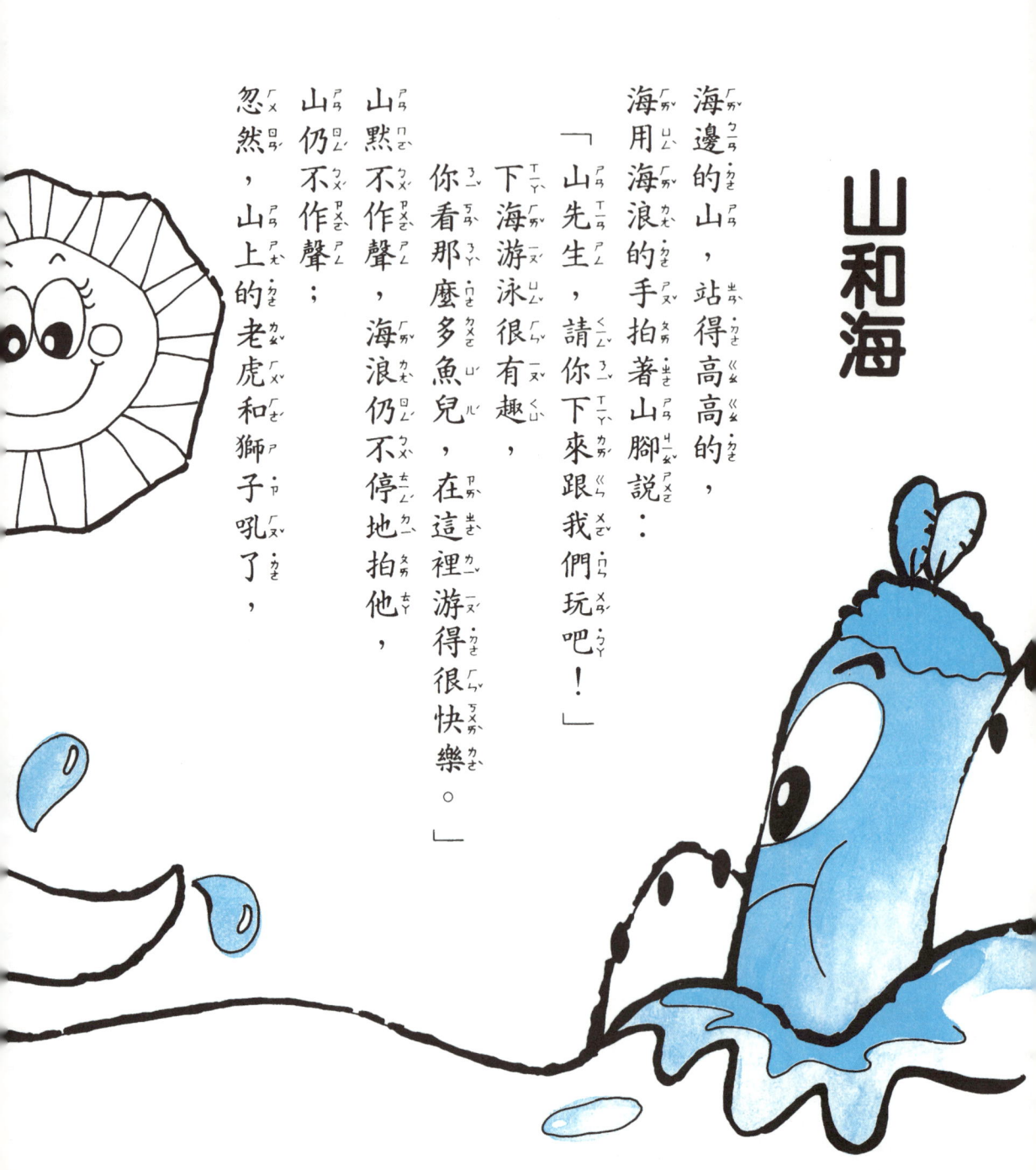

海邊的山,站得高高的,
海用海浪的手拍著山腳說:
「山先生,請你下來跟我們玩吧!
下海游泳很有趣,
你看那麼多魚兒,在這裡游得很快樂。」
山仍不作聲;
山默不作聲,海浪仍不停地拍他,
山仍不作聲;
忽然,山上的老虎和獅子吼了,

他們吼著說：

「海小姐喲！請妳別叫我們的山大哥去游泳了，因為我們不會游泳，會溺死的，不然，請妳的魚、蝦小弟妹們上山來玩，他們也會乾死。」

天公聽了，哈哈大笑說：

「天生萬物，各有其性，不可勉強啊！」

——「高市兒童」第九期 79年7月

The Sea and the Mountain

The mountain stands high by the seaside.
The waves beating the foot of the mountain say,
"Mr. Mountain, would you please come down to play with us?
It is fun to come down to swim and
See many fish swim happily."
The mountain remains silent, and the waves keep beating.
The mountain still remains silent.
All of a sudden, tigers and lions on the mountain begin to roar,

Saying, "Miss Sea, don't tell Brother Mountain to swim.
We cannot swim; we will drown.
Why don't you ask your fish and shrimps to climb the mountain
    and play with us?
They will dry up and die."
The Heavenly Father laughingly says,
"Everything on earth has its place.
No one can tell it to do anything against its nature!"

    —Kaohsiung Children' Journal, #9, July 1990

山和海

—兒童文學 78年5月

山是海的好朋友
山高高地站着
靜靜地常年守衞大海
大海也不停地唱着海浪之歌
給山欣賞
又開着無數美麗的浪花
給山欣賞

The Sea and the Mountain

The mountain is a good friend of the sea.
The mountain stands high,
Silently guarding the sea.
The sea never stops singing songs of sea waves
For the mountain to enjoy.
The sea produces many waves like beautiful flowers
For the mountain to see.

—Children's Literature, #7, May 1989.

海浪

海浪是大海的花朵
大海是最富生命力的巨樹
能夠日日夜夜開花
年年月月開花
我們也要充實生命力
才能開出無數美麗的花朵

——「兒童文學」第七輯 78年5月

Sea waves

Sea waves are like beautiful flowers.
The sea is like a gigantic tree, so energetic
That it produces flowers day and night,
Year in and year out.
One must be as energetic and full of life force
To produce as many flowers.

—Children's Literature, #7, May 1989.

春天

春天是個美麗的姑娘
穿着艷麗的衣裳
和綠色的草鞋
吹走冷冬的天氣
表演春之頌給我們欣賞

—兒童文學 78年5月

Spring

Spring is like a beautiful young lady,
Wearing multicolored dresses and
Green sandals.
Spring drives away the cold winter and
Sings songs for us to enjoy.

—Children's Literature, #7, May 1989.

夏天

―兒童文學 78年5月

夏天是個脾氣暴躁的演員
每天表演都帶着火熱的太陽
晒得人人滿身大汗
無心欣賞

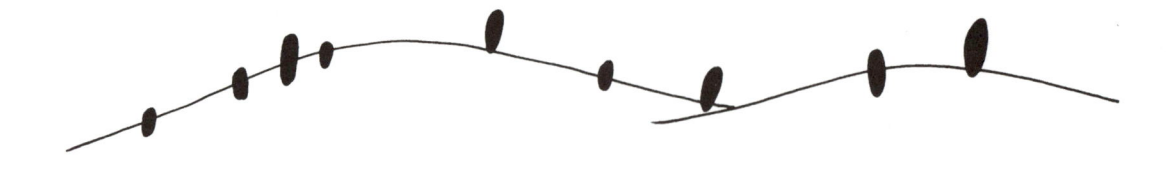

Summer

Summer is like a grumpy actor.
Every day he carries the fiery sun, playing his drama.
Under the sun, everybody is perspiring and
Has no mood for the drama.

—Children's Literature, #7, May 1989.

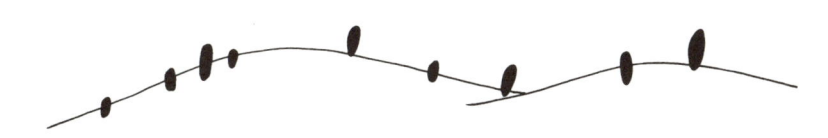

秋天

秋天是個更年期的半徐老娘
動不動就發脾氣
把許多樹葉打落滿地

——兒童文學 78年5月

Autumn

Autumn is like a middle-aged lady in her period of menopause.
She is always in a fit of ill temper,
Shaking the leaves to fall on the ground.

—Children's Literature, #7, May 1989.

冬天

冬天是個白衣姑娘
自己喜歡穿雪白的衣裳
又賜給大地一件冰冷的白色大衣
穿得跟自己一模一樣
穿了幾個月後
才換花花綠綠的衣裳

——兒童文學 78年5月

Winter

Winter looks like a young lady dressed in white.
She so likes to be dressed in white
That she wants the earth to be dressed in cold,
white clothes, too.
Like her, the earth is dressed in white.
In a matter of a few months,
The earth would change into colorful clothes.

—Children's Literature, #7, May 1989.

秋天

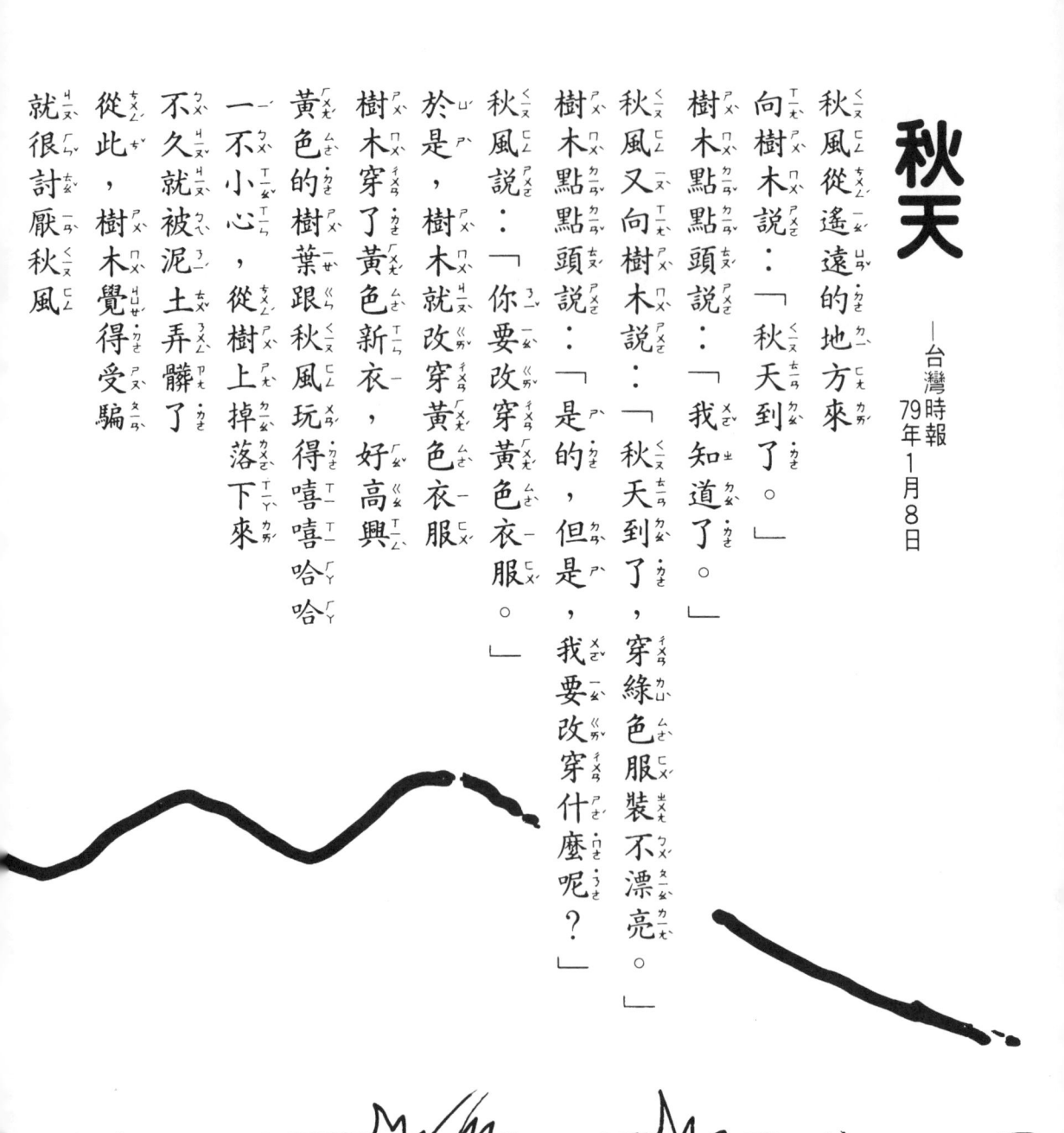

—台灣時報 79年1月8日

秋風從遙遠的地方來

向樹木說:「秋天到了。」

樹木點點頭說:「我知道了。」

秋風又向樹木說:「秋天到了,穿綠色服裝不漂亮。」

樹木點點頭說:「是的,但是,我要改穿什麼呢?」

秋風說:「你要改穿黃色衣服。」

於是,樹木就改穿黃色衣服

樹木穿了黃色新衣,好高興

黃色的樹葉跟秋風玩得嘻嘻哈哈

一不小心,從樹上掉落下來

不久就被泥土弄髒了

從此,樹木覺得受騙

就很討厭秋風

108

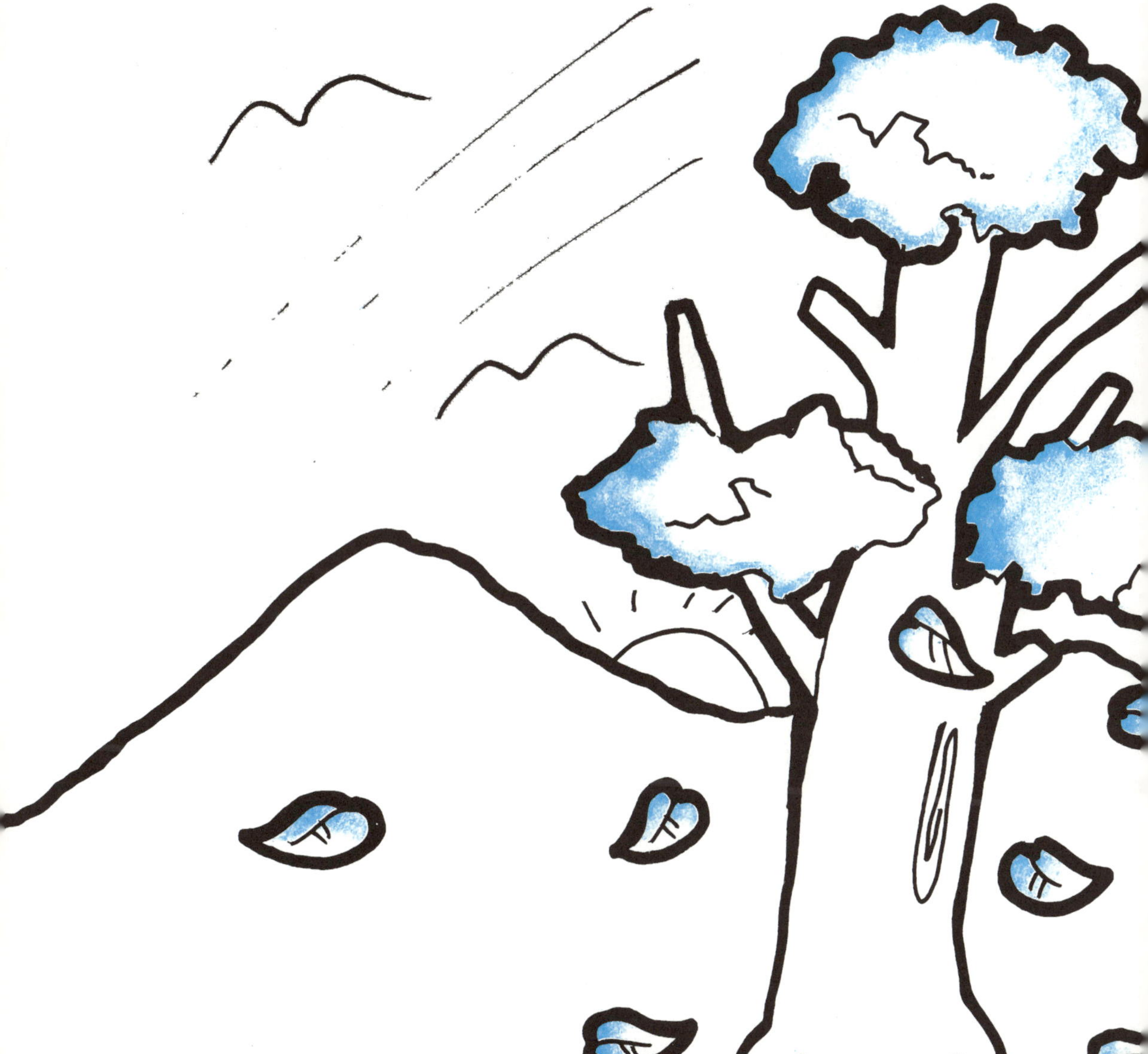

Autumn

Autumn wind coming from faraway places
Announces to the trees, "Autumn is here."
The trees nodding say, "I know."
Autumn says, "Your green clothing is not beautiful."
The trees ask, "Yes, but in what color should I be dressed?"
Autumn answers, "In yellow."
So the trees change into yellow clothes and are happy.
The yellow trees play with autumn wind gleefully.
Accidentally, leaves fall from the trees, and
The fallen leaves are dirtied on the ground in no time.
The trees feel cheated and hate autumn wind.

　　—Taiwan Times, January 8, 1990.

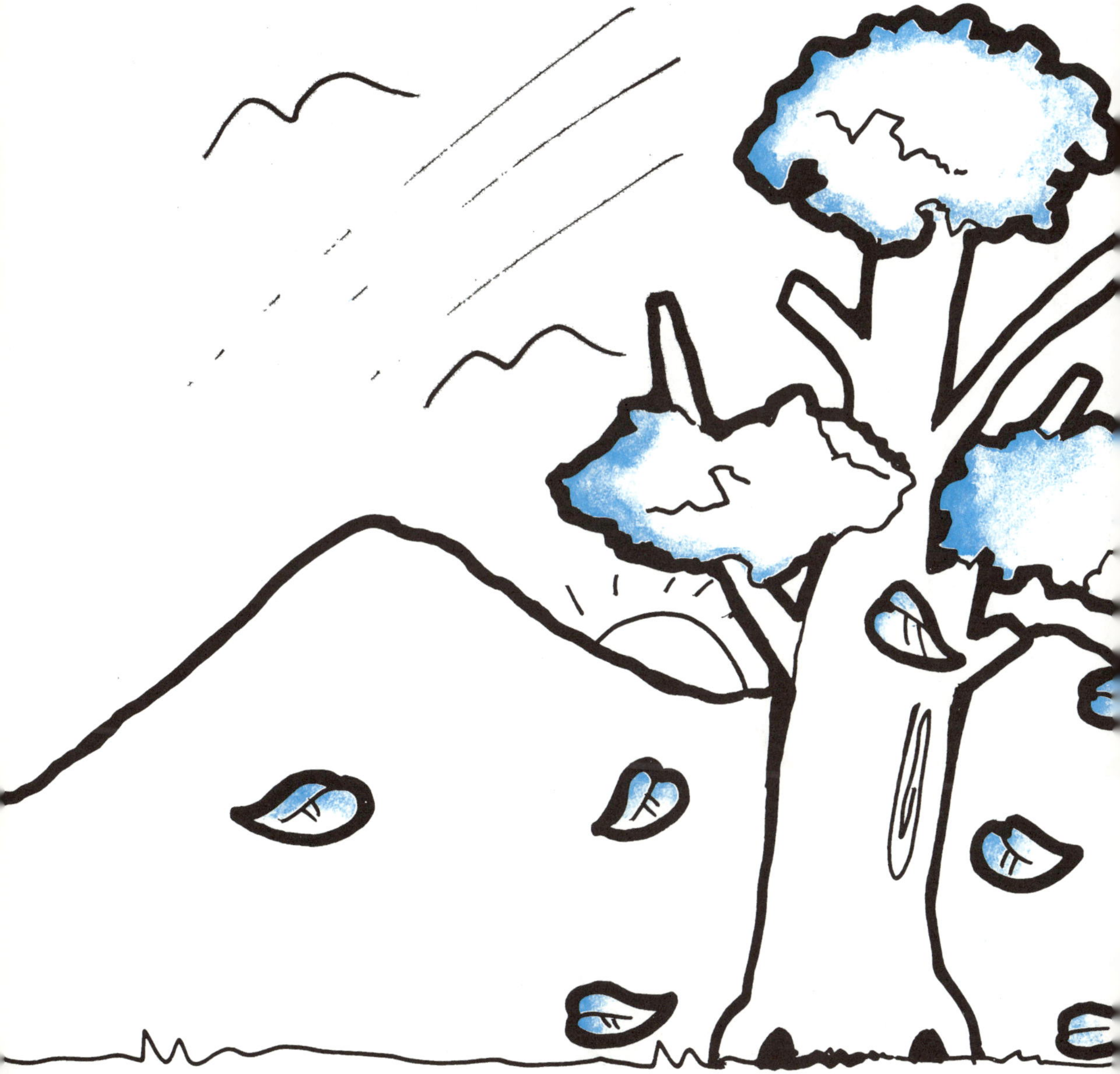

颱風

妳像瘋狂的潑辣婦,
拿着大掃帚和水桶,
大吵、大鬧、水亂倒、掃帚亂揮,
房屋掃破了,樹木摧倒了,
她才怒氣冲冲的走開。

颱風嫂啊!
我們沒有罵妳,
也沒有得罪妳,
妳為什麼要發那麼大的脾氣,
搞得我們慘兮兮?

——民眾日報 78年12月25日

A Typhoon

You are like a crazy shrew
Carrying a big broom and a big bucket.
Crazily and noisily, you empty the bucket everywhere.
Houses are destroyed and trees are rooted.
Then, you angrily go away.
Sister Typhoon,
I have not cursed you,
Nor have I offended you.
Why should you be in such a fit of ill temper
To have brought us such miseries?

—People's Daily, December 25, 1989.

下雨

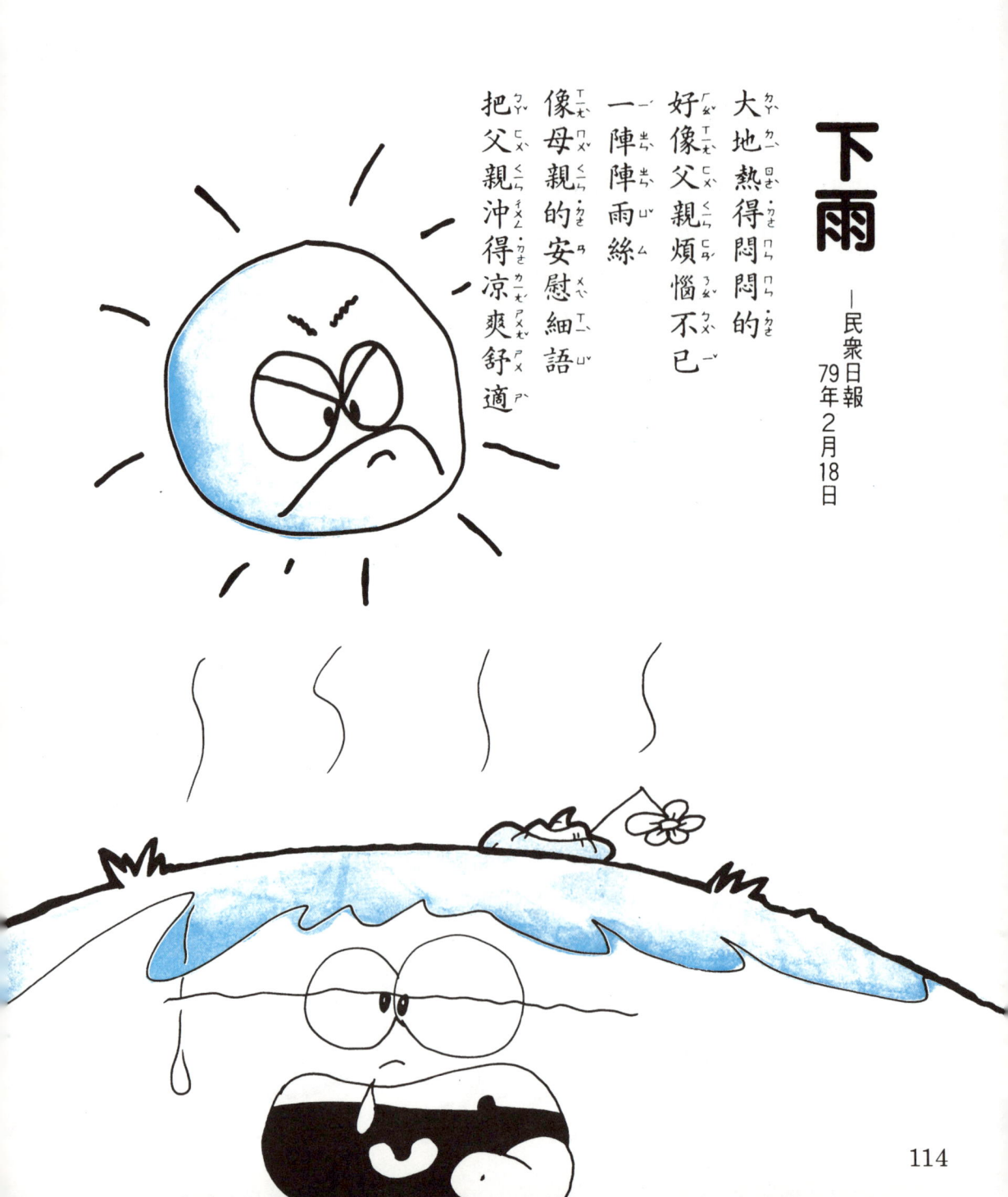

——民眾日報 79年2月18日

大地熱得悶悶的
好像父親煩惱不已
一陣陣雨絲
像母親的安慰細語
把父親沖得涼爽舒適

Raining

It is hot on earth,
The earth being like my father troubled and upset.
It rains for a while.
The raindrops are like my mother's soothing whispers
Making my father calm down and be comfortable.

—People's Daily, February 18, 1990. Rain

雨

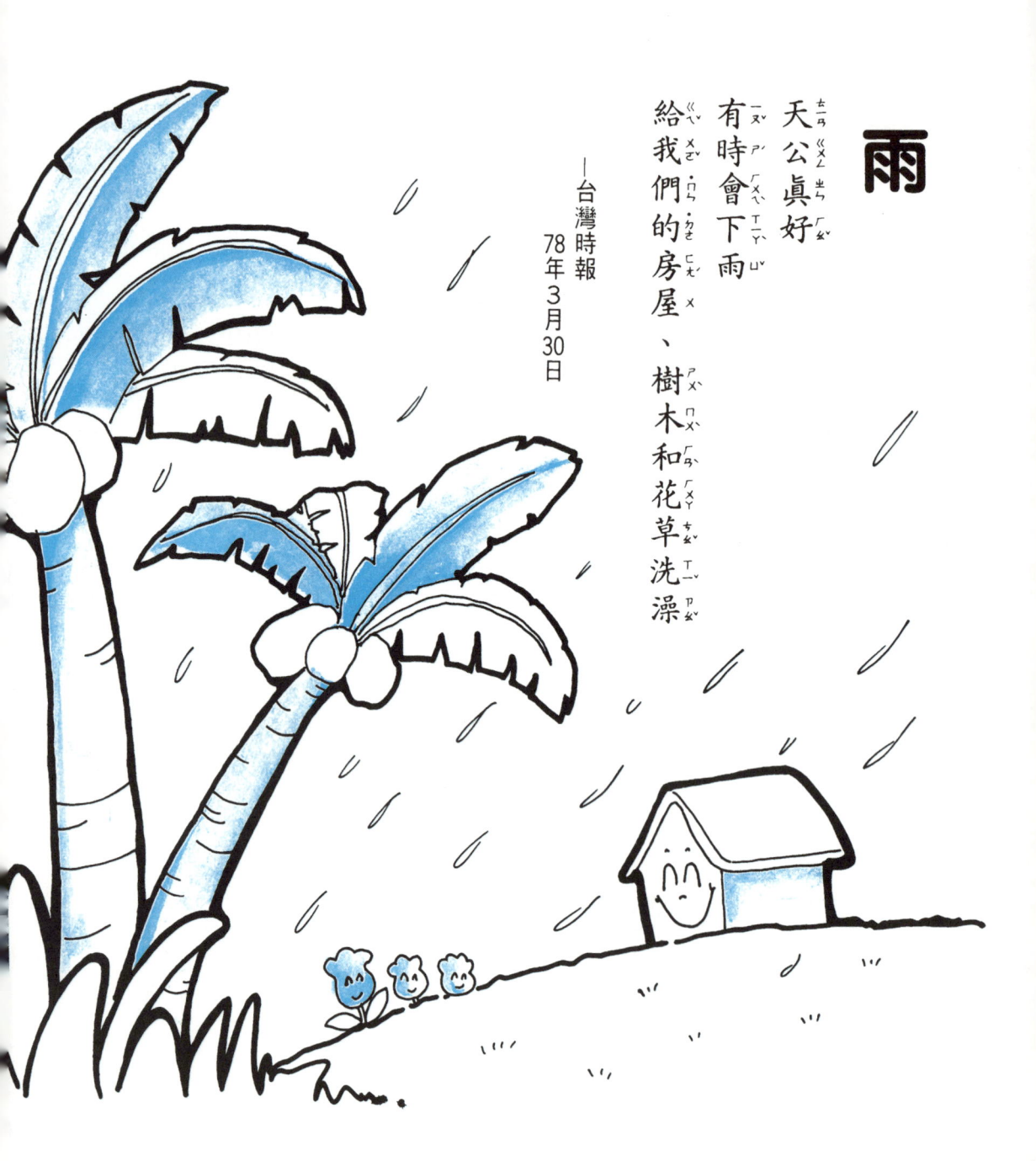

天公真好
有時會下雨
給我們的房屋、樹木和花草洗澡

—台灣時報 78年3月30日

Rain

The Heavenly Father is so good
That it rains sometimes,
Bathing trees, grass, flowers and our houses.
—Taiwan Times, March 30, 1989.

雨

—「幼稚園雜誌」第二期 77年3月

雨是愛哭的孩子
自己哭得滿身濕濕的
還要淋濕別人
太陽公公出來後
她就不敢哭了

Rain

Rain is like a crying child.
He cries and gets wet.
He also gets others soaked through and through.
As soon as Grandpa Sun appears,
He stops crying.

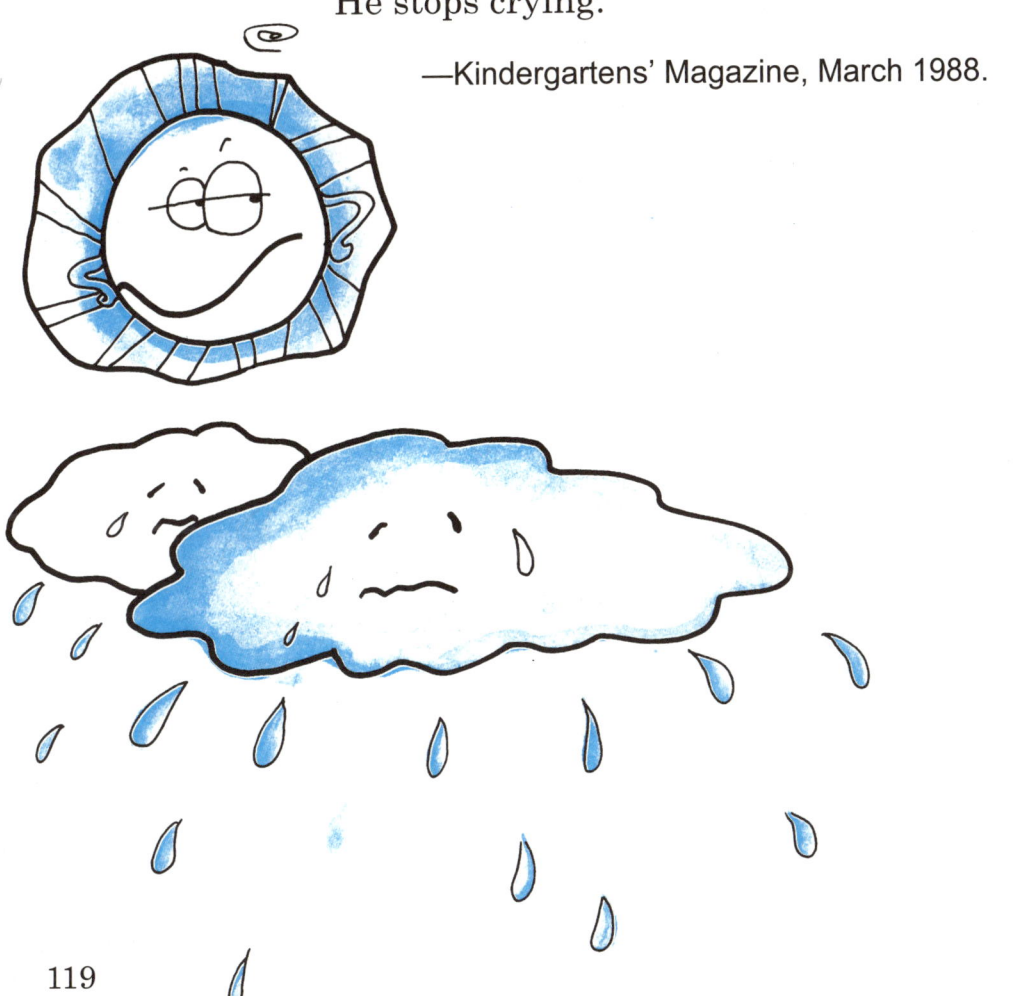

—Kindergartens' Magazine, March 1988.

動物園

動物園真好玩
老虎、獅子、猴子樣樣看
走著看,走著玩
還有羚羊,大象看不完
走著看,走著玩
不知不覺全看完

——台灣時報 77年11月8日

At a Zoo

It's fun to be at a zoo.
There are tigers, lions, and monkeys.
Walking around, we have fun.
There are also antelopes and elephants and others.
Walking around, we have fun.
Before we know it, we have seen all.

—Taiwan Times, November 8, 1988.

海天相連

青青的天
藍藍的海
海連天
天連海
海天相連
連又連
把我快樂的心田
連向海
連向天
連連連

——七賢國小「學校與家庭」
77年12月

The Sea and the Sky

The blue sky and
The azure sea are linked together.
The sea and the sky,
The sky and the sea—
They are both linked together,
Linking and linking.
My happy heart is linked to the sea, and
Is also linked to the sky.
There is linking and again
There is linking.

　　—School and Family Journal, Qishian Primary
　　　School, December 1988.

稻草人

我是稻草人
站在稻禾中
不怕雨，不怕風
不怕冷，不怕熱
站在稻禾中
我是稻草人
不吃草，不吃飯
天天會做工

我是稻草人
站在稻禾中
沒有耳朵，沒有眼睛
鳥兒看了心忡忡

我是稻草人
站在稻禾中
沒有嘴巴，沒有鼻子
是農夫的好長工

―台灣新聞報 77年9月5日

A Scarecrow

I am a scarecrow,
Standing in the rice paddies.
I am not afraid of coldness, nor of hotness.
I am not afraid of rain, nor of wind.
I am a scarecrow,
Standing in the rice paddies.
I don't have to eat grass, nor to eat rice.
Yet, I work all day long.

I am a scarecrow,
Standing in the rice paddies.
I don't have ears, nor eyes.
Yet, the birds are afraid of me.
I am a scarecrow,
Standing in the rice paddies.
I don't have a mouth, nor a nose.
Yet, I am a good farmhand.

—Taiwan Newspaper, September 5, 1988.

春風

春風輕聲細語的，
向樹木說：「我像維他命給你發芽生長。」
向花木說：「我就像香水引發你長出芬芳的花朵。」
樹木和花木就乖乖的讓春風吹著，
像小孩乖乖地給慈母搖著搖籃，
快樂地長大，
快樂地開花。

——七賢國小「學校與家庭」
77年12月

Spring breezes

Spring breezes say softly
To the trees, "I come as vitamin for your sprouts to grow."
Spring breezes say softly
To the flower plants,
    "I come as a perfume to help grow your fragrant flowers."
The trees and the flower plants obediently stand there and
    receive the breezes,
Like babies in the cradles swung by their kind mothers.
They grow happily, and bloom happily.

        — School and Family Journal,
          Qishian Primary School, December 1988.

河流

水兒流
水兒流
水兒流又流
早上流
晚上流
日日夜夜流

——七賢國小「學校與家庭」
77年12月

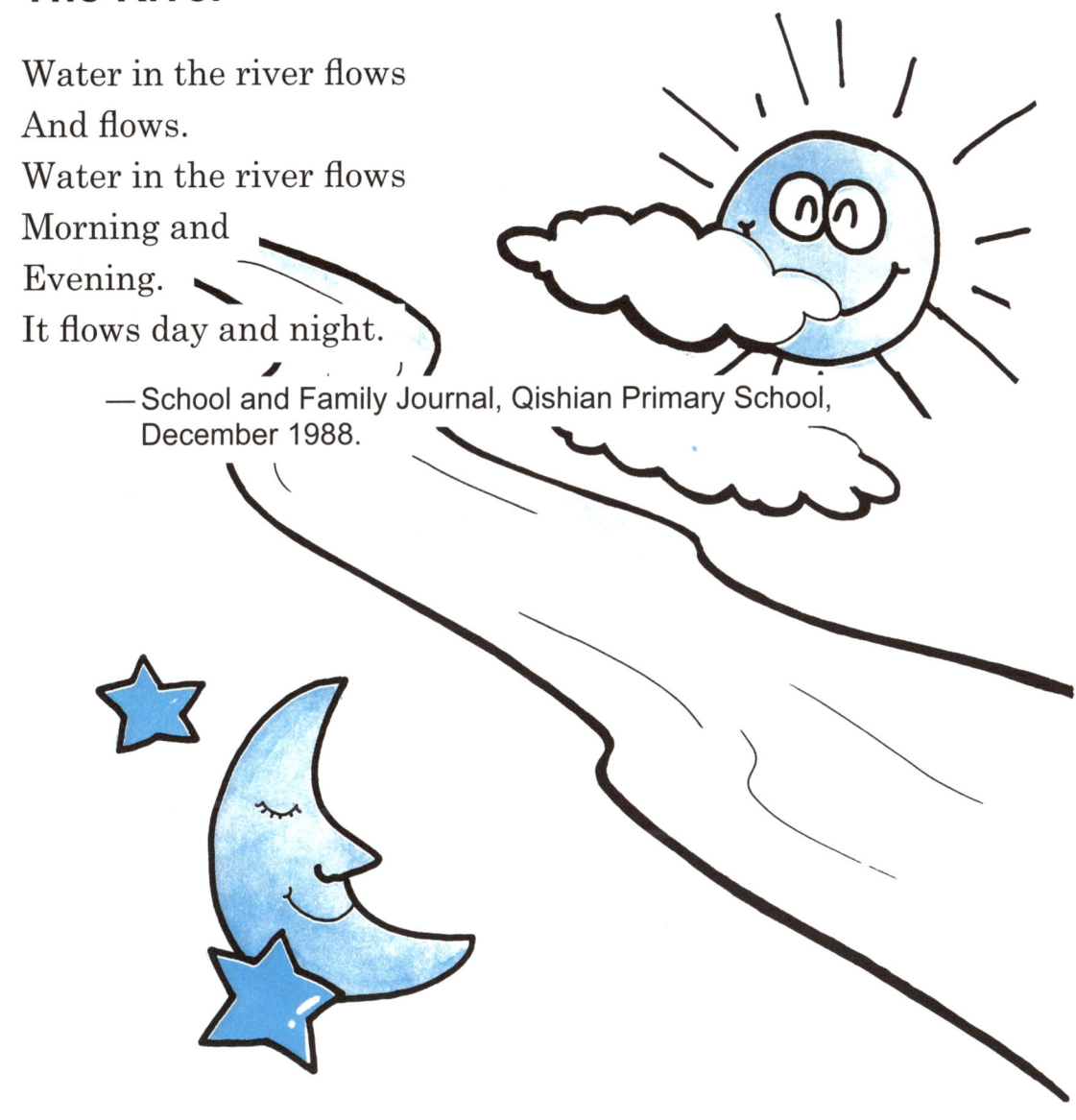

The River

Water in the river flows
And flows.
Water in the river flows
Morning and
Evening.
It flows day and night.

—School and Family Journal, Qishian Primary School,
December 1988.

木馬

——七賢國小「學校與家庭」77年12月

木馬搖呀搖
木馬不會跑
木馬搖呀搖
愈搖愈逍遙

The Wooden Horse

The wooden horse rocks back and forth.

The wooden horse cannot run away.

The wooden horse can only rock back and forth.

The more it rocks the happier it is.

— School and Family Journal, Qishian Primary School, December 1988.

蹺蹺板

你一蹺我一降
我一蹺你一降
蹺降蹺降
像起伏的海浪

—七賢國小「學校與家庭」
77年12月

The Seesaw

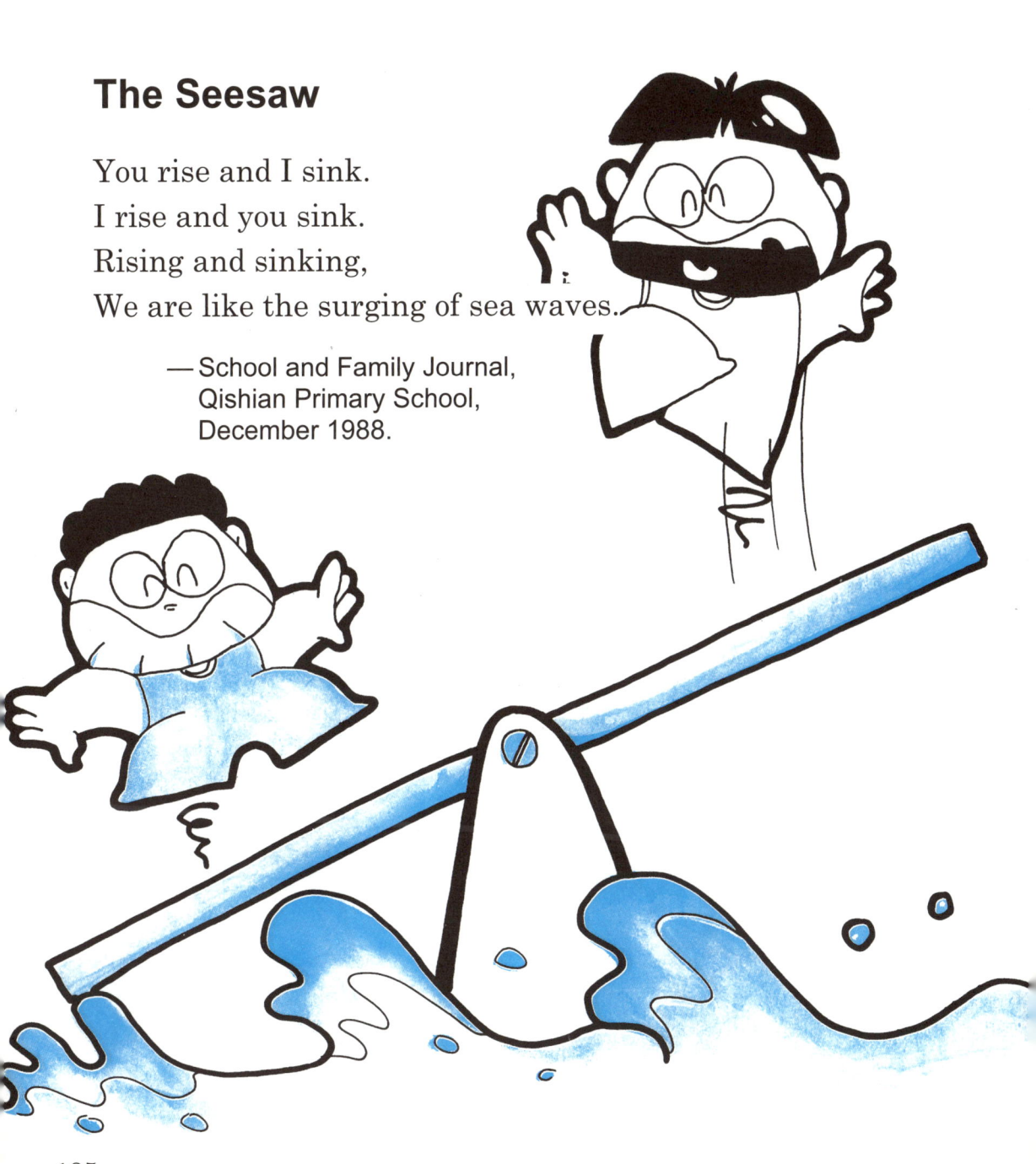

You rise and I sink.
I rise and you sink.
Rising and sinking,
We are like the surging of sea waves.

—School and Family Journal,
Qishian Primary School,
December 1988.

盪秋千

盪鞦韆像搖籃
一搖一擺像鐘擺
搖呀搖
擺呀擺
擺著我們的喜笑

——七賢國小「學校與家庭」
77年12月

Playing a Swing

Playing the swing is like swinging in a cradle.
The swinging is like that of a pendulum.
Swinging and swinging, we giggle and are happy.

— School and Family Journal, Qishian Primary School, December 1988.

天空的花朵

白雲是天空的花朵
長在天空的大樹上
一朵一朵
大大小小
各式各樣的花朵
開了又開
謝了又謝
在天上飄來飄去
讓我們看得眼花撩亂

——台灣新聞報 77年11月7日

Flowers in the Sky

White clouds are flowers in the sky.
They grow on a big tree in the sky.
A flower here and another there,
Big ones and small ones.
All kinds of flowers blossom and fade,
Fade and blossom.
They float here and there in the sky.
We become dazzled watching the changes of
    the flowers in the sky.

—Taiwan Times, November 7, 1988.

車輛是都市的魚

都市有許多街路
街路是都市的河流
車輛是都市的魚
在街路上走來走去
就像魚兒在河裡游來游去
魚兒守規則
游來游去無車禍
而我們的車輛常常不守規則
所以常常有車禍

Vehicles Are Like Fish in the City

There are many streets in the city.
The streets are like rivers.
Vehicles are like fish in the city
Running here and there.
They are like fish swimming here and there.
Swimming, the fish have to observe traffic rules, and
There would not be accidents.
However, our vehicles do not always observe rules.
That's why there are always accidents.

蝴蝶是會飛的花朵

蝴蝶是花兒的好友
花兒一開蝴蝶多
漂亮的花兒站著
等待蝴蝶來相會

蝴蝶好漂亮
蝴蝶是會飛的花朵
站著微笑的花朵
歡迎會飛的花朵
一起做朋友

——兒童的雜誌
79年5月

Butterflies are Flying Flowers

Butterflies are flowers' good friends.
The blossoming of flowers would invite many butterflies.
Beautiful flowers stand there
Waiting for the butterflies to come.
Butterflies are beautiful.
They are flying flowers.
The smiling flowers stand there
To welcome the butterflies which seem to be flying flowers.
Flowers and butterflies get together as friends.

    —Children's Magazine, May 1990.

房屋是都市的森林

是都市的森林
一間間的公寓
一棟棟的大樓

這是鋼筋水泥的森林
我們住在硬硬的方形巨林裡
毫無一綠意
只有混凝土的氣味
只看白色的牆壁和單調的壁紙
天空變矮了，變窄了
害得我們成為四眼田雞

都市的森林
沒有花木的芳香
也無清新的空氣
只有怪氣、炭氣和臭氣
使我們喪失了天真自然的靈氣

——「滿天星」第13期
79年6月

Houses Are the Forest in the City

Tall buildings and
Apartment houses are
The forest of the city.
This is a forest of steel and concrete.
We live in a stiff, hard, square, gigantic forest,
Without greenery.
There is only the smell of concrete.
Indoors, we see only white walls and monotonous wall paper.
The sky seems to grow lower and narrower.
Many of us have become myopic.

The forest in the city has no fragrance of trees and flowers.
There is no fresh air,
Only strange air, brutal air, and smelly air.
We have lost our innocence and natural-born quality.

   —Mantian Xing Magazine, #13, June 1990.

刷牙歌

起牀後漱漱口
飯後要刷牙
睡前又刷牙
牙刷向牙斜斜擦
四十五度斜斜插
來回旋轉斜斜刷
咬合面上垂直刷
裡外都要刷
沒有蛀牙笑哈哈
牙齒健康身體佳

——「兒童的雜誌」第21期
77年6月1日

The Song for Tooth-brushing

After getting up in the morning, the first thing you have to do is wash your mouth.
After having breakfast, you brush your teeth.
Before going to bed at night, you should brush your teeth again.
The steps of brushing your teeth: holding the toothbrush obliquely to the teeth
In a 45-degree manner and brushing the teeth back and forth.
You have also to brush the occlusal surfaces of the teeth,
Inside and out.
Brushing your teeth correctly, you will not get decayed ones.
With healthy teeth, you will grow strong and be happy.

—Children's Magazine, June 1, 1988.

爸爸媽媽的皺紋

爸爸的皺紋
是賺錢的痕跡
媽媽的皺紋
是燒飯洗衣的痕跡
我沒有皺紋
因為我不會賺錢、燒飯、洗衣
我只會讀書
我要用書壓平爸爸媽媽的皺紋

──全國兒童 77年5月22日

Parents' Wrinkles

The wrinkles on my father's face are
The record of his hard working for earning money, and
Those on my mother's face,
The record of her having done a lot of household chores.
I do not have wrinkles
Because I do not earn money, cook, nor do laundry.
The only thing I should do is studying.
I would like to use my high scores in my studies to iron out their wrinkles.

—All-nation Children's Magazine, May 22, 1988.

蠶絲

蠶吃了綠色的桑葉之後
吐出細細白白的可愛蠶絲
給我們編織新衣

而我們吃了白白的米飯之後
吐出黑字的詩
留傳於世

—美國世界日報 79年6月21日

Silk

After having eaten green mulberry leaves, silkworms
Produce white, soft, lovable silk
For us to weave our new clothes.
On the other hand, we eat white rice and
Produce poetry in black ideograms
For the readers around the world to read.

—The American World Daily, June 21, 1990.

愛吃糖的螞蟻

小小螞蟻在吃糖，
一塊糖菓被分光，
却不見你們刷牙。
不知你們蛀了多少牙，
才能把全部糖菓吃光？

Ants that Love Eating Sugar

Little ants are eating sugar,
One lump after another.
I do not see you brush your teeth.
I do not know how many decayed teeth there will be
Before you eat up all the sugar.

愛生氣的蓮霧

你為什麼愈成熟
臉就愈紅
原來你在生氣
有人要採你吃

156

An Angry Wax Apple

Why does your face become redder
As you grow more mature?
Oh, I see. You are angry
Because people are going to pick you and eat you!

萬能的電話

電話嘵嘵響
朋友有話講
長線接嘴巴
千里可傳話

The Omnipotent Telephone

The telephone rings.
Friends are going to talk over it.
The long wire is connecting two mouths, and
There will be communication.

美麗的月亮

月亮光光
月亮圓圓
月亮高掛天空上
畫了美麗的圓圈
自己塗上了彩色
成為美麗的畫面

The Beautiful Moon

The moon is round and is
Luminous.
The moon hangs high up in the sky.
It looks like a disc
Painted with many colors by herself.
The moon-lit night is a beautiful picture.

愛玩的星星

星星亮晶晶
星星點點明
逍遙天空上
一笑一笑
一唱一唱
一笑一笑
玩到天亮

The Playful Stars

The stars are shiny.
The sky is dotted with little shiny stars.
The stars seem to be wandering there,
Laughing and singing,
Singing and laughing
Till the dawn of the day.

愛唱歌的春風

春風輕輕吹
草兒頻點頭
東搖西擺在唱歌
大家都快樂

Spring Breezes that Love Singing

Spring breezes blow softly, and
The grass keeps nodding and shaking.
Nodding and shaking, spring breezes and the grass are singing.
Seeing all this, we are happy.

小氣的白雲

白雲飄在天空上
像許多棉花糖
飄來飄去
不給人吃
最後送給太陽公公吃

Stingy White Clouds

White clouds float in the sky,
Like cotton candies.
They float here and there,
Not allowing us to eat them.
Rather, they are eaten up by Grandpa Sun.

雨給地球洗澡

雨嘩啦嘩啦
像一群小鴨呱呱呱
日日夜夜吵
太陽被吵走了
星星也躲起來睡覺
原來他們忙着給地球洗澡

Rain Is Bathing the Earth

Raindrops keep falling down
Like the quacking of little ducks
Day and night.
The sun hides away because of the noises.
The stars also hide away to sleep.
Rain is bathing the earth.

山是天空的守護神

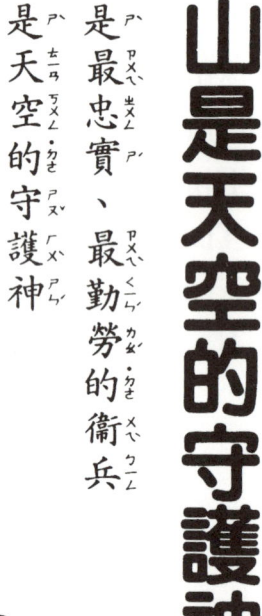

山是最忠實、最勤勞的衛兵
山是天空的守護神
他站在地球上
白天看太陽
晚上守月亮
天天在站崗

The Mountain Is the Guardian Angel of the Sky

The mountain is a faithful, diligent guard.
The mountain is the guardian angel of the sky.
It stands firmly on earth.
At day, it watches the sun, and
At night, it guards the moon.
It stands guard day in and day out.

喜歡抓東西的椰子樹

高高的椰子樹
舉起長長的手臂
白天想抓太陽
晚上想抓月亮
結果什麼都沒抓到
只抓到一陣一陣的風
一滴滴的雨
自己玩耍
自得樂趣

——台灣新聞報 79年9月2日

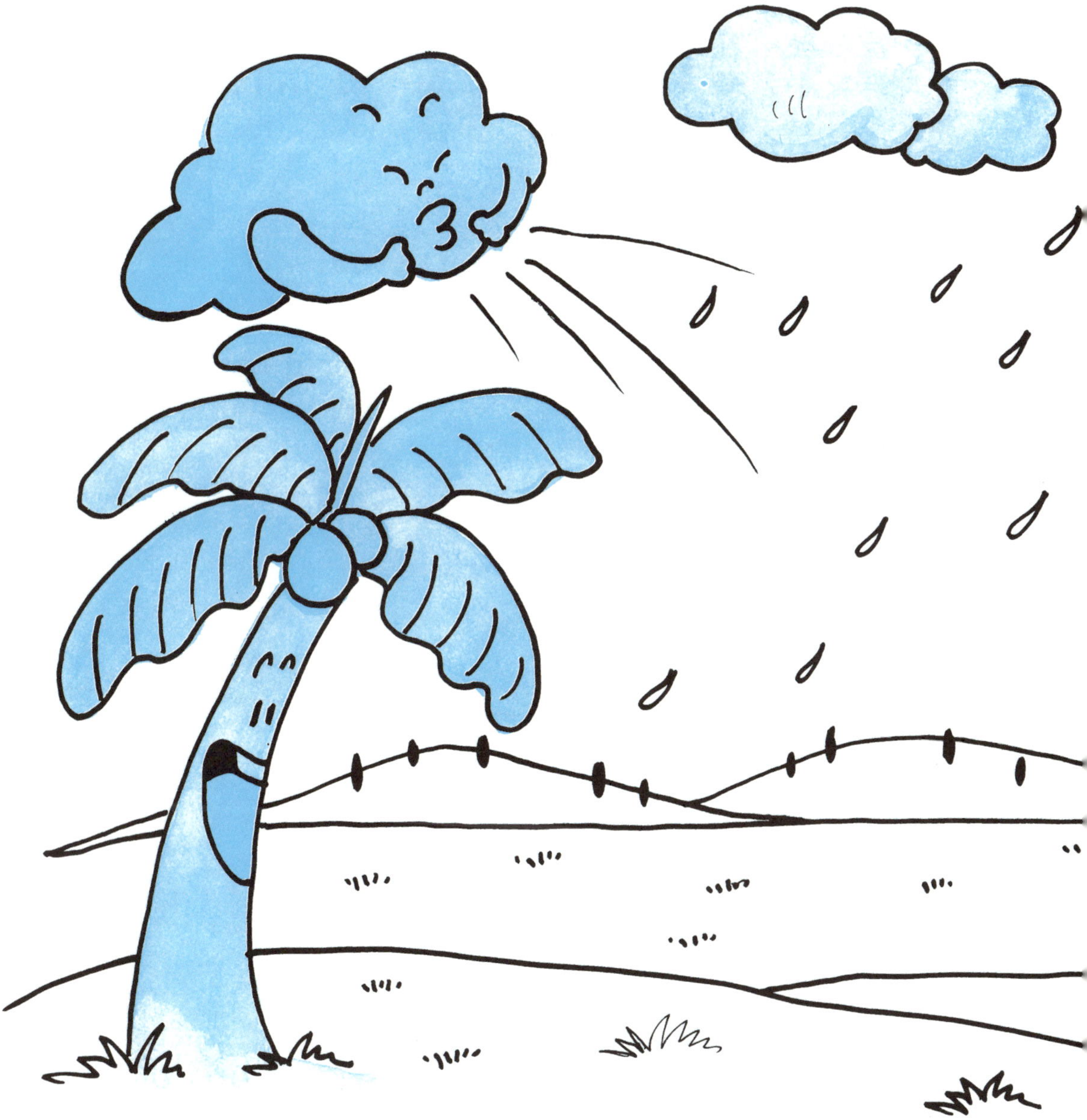

Palm Trees that Like to Catch Things

The tall palm trees
Raise their long arms
To catch the sun during the day and
To catch the moon at night.
But, eventually, they have caught neither.

They have caught only some wind and some raindrops.
The tall palm trees seem to be playing by themselves and
Enjoying themselves.

—Taiwan Times, September 2, 1990.

蜻蜓是一架小飛機

青草河邊蜻蜓飛
蜻蜓像美麗的小飛機
不加汽油
也能飛來飛去
真有趣

我如果能夠變為小螞蟻
坐在蜻蜓上
駕駛小蜻蜓
在原野飛來飛去
該多有趣

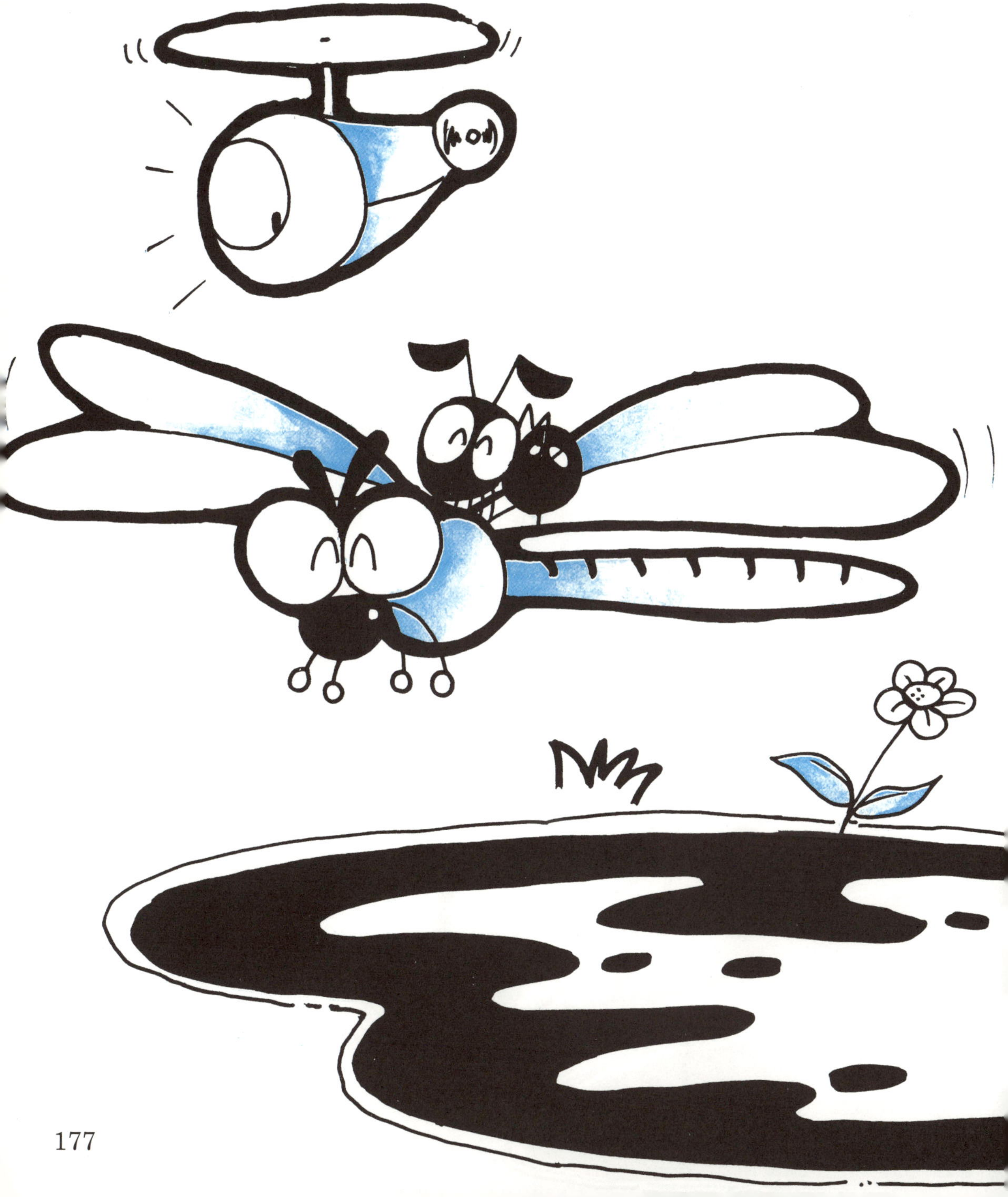

Dragonflies Are Like Airplanes

Over the meadow by the river,
Dragonflies fly like little beautiful airplanes.
They do not need gasoline.
It is fun to see
Them fly here and there.
I wish that I could be a little ant
To ride on a dragonfly,
And steer it
To fly over the field here and there.
Then, how fun it would be !

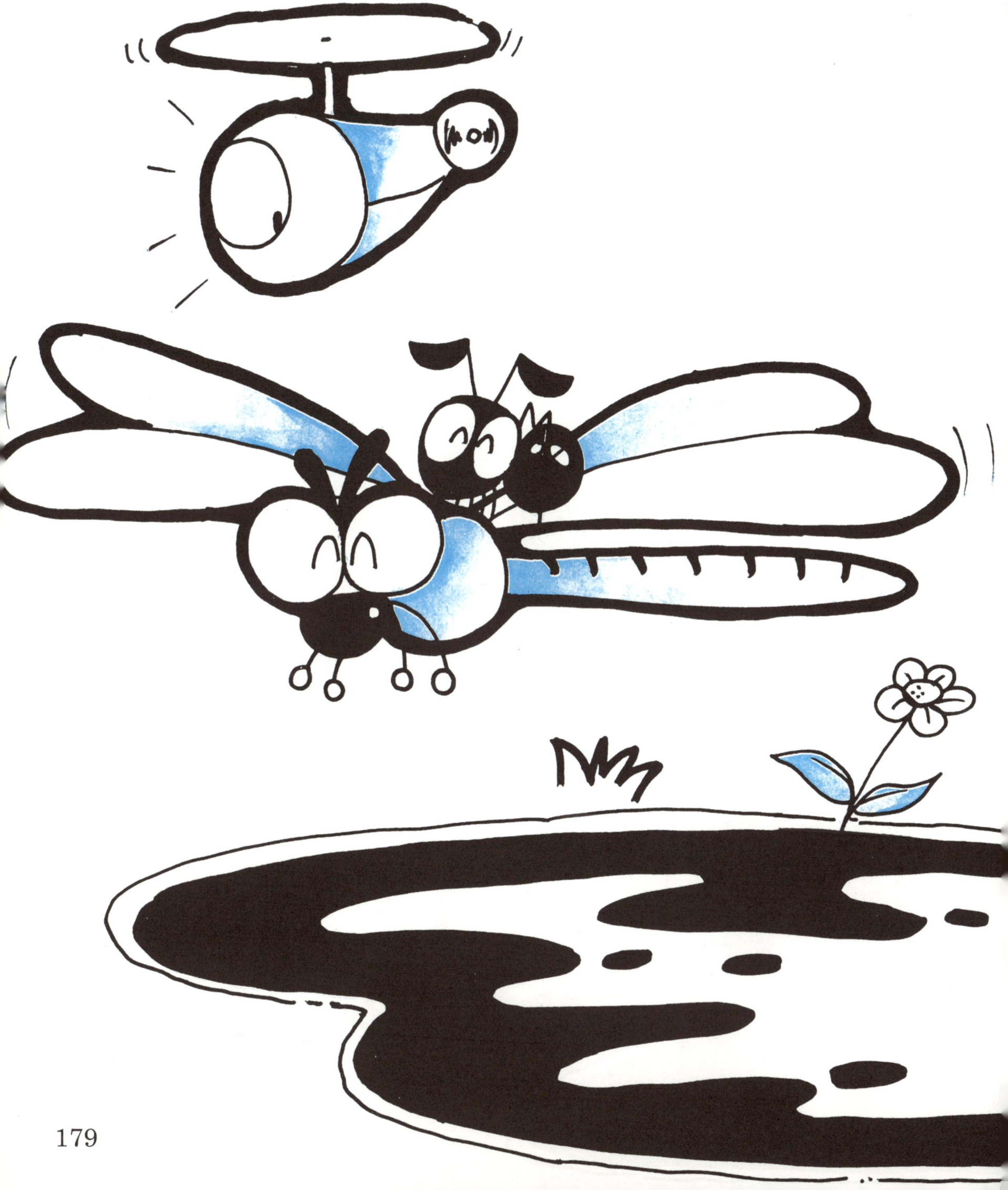

沙白與童詩

阿紅

這沙白是海峽彼岸的。一下子寄我七本著作。我先看的兒童詩。兒童世界，我總是滿懷興趣。

沙白是名牙醫，又是名詩人。為成人寫詩的人，往往不寫兒童詩。縱寫，也是偶而，沙白却是正經寫的。他是「全人生」詩人。

他有一套兒童詩論。

他定義兒童詩為：「具有兒童靈魂及兒童意識的詩。也就是在感覺和知覺上，對事物及其意象之表現，容易為兒童心靈感應的詩。」我看這定義比把「嬰兒奶粉」定義為「嬰兒吃的奶粉」之類要能說明兒童詩的特點。

他重視兒童詩的效用。兒童，祖國的未來，人類的未來，為兒童寫詩當然要重視效用。沙白歸納成：「①使兒童認識更多的文字，並活用更多的文字，使之生命化和鮮活化。②培養兒童天真的童心，使之更純潔可愛。③啟發兒童的想像力，使他對自己及家庭、社會和四周的事務更關心。④培育兒童更深厚的同情心，成為社會的好人。⑤增進兒童的知識，薰陶兒童美育和德育的心靈，增加生活的趣味和快樂。⑥引發和培養兒童對文藝的興趣。

⑦引導兒童的心理和情緒走向正常的軌道。

⑧兒童寫童詩，可以在潛意識及意識裡，確立其存在之意義和價值，並展現其人生的理想。」設想是周到的。我感覺在現在這個地球，還得強調愛祖國、愛人民、愛勞動、愛科學的教育。一海阻隔，意識自有差異。

我有三個孫兒女，免不了要在買「飛機」、「汽車人」的時候，也買兒歌兒童詩。我的印象：理性強而童趣弱，幾乎全是民歌體。民歌體有民歌體的好處，三、五、七言，瑯瑯上口。沙白的兒童詩富有兒童趣味、兒童想像；重視智育、德育、美育，內容寬闊；使用有節奏感的口語，比較自由。我念一些給冬冬、南南聽，孩子聽得小眼烏亮。比如《河：「河流只有一條腸子／婉婉蠕動着／她吃得不多／永遠是苗條細長的」。比如《瀑布》：「遠遠的山上有一匹瀑布／像一塊長長的毛巾／飄在天上／玩來玩去／不久就被太陽吃得光光。」有的詞彙，那是給山洗澡用的。」比如《白雲》：「白雲像棉花糖／孩子是生些，一解釋便理解，孩子也多認了字。孩子聽了詩，爭着要書。我這爺爺只有割愛。

台灣教育界兒童文學界重視沙白的奉獻。有的說：「語言輕快活潑，有節奏感。想像豐富、天真有趣，有趣味性也有空靈的意境。」有的說：「很能抓住孩子的思想和對事物的觀察。」有的小學用作補充教材。

也許是因為寫兒童詩，他日常注意收集孩子偶然冒出的「詩語」。沙白二子一女，常常妙語如珠：「月亮像指甲」。「把山用刀子剖開，像剖西瓜一樣，車子就開過去了。」實在有趣。不了解童心，是喚不起童心的。我的小孫子也常有這類詩語，可惜我僅讚了幾句，沒有記錄。

沙白小我十三歲，也四十六了，竟有一顆童心。我羨慕。

（作者為中國大陸著名作家及文學評論家）。

——原載大陸「海南日報」一九八九年十月卅一日

Sar Po and His Children's Poetry

—A Mainland Chinese writer, A Hong

I received seven books sent by Sar Po from Taiwan. Among them, I picked up a collection of children's poetry. I am always excited about children's world.

Sar Po is a dentist in Taiwan. He is also a well-known poet. He who writes only poetry for the general readers would rarely write children's poetry. If he does write children's poetry, it is a rare thing for him to happen. Sar Po is such a poet, writing poetry for adults and children alike. He is one who pays attention to all aspects of human life.

He has his own poetics about children's poetry writing. He defines children's poetry as containing "children's spirit and children's consciousness. The respresentation of things and their images in the poetry would appeal to the children's mind." It seems to me that the definition would be better than defining babies' milk simply as milk drunk by babies.

He places emphasis on the effects of children's poetry.

The purpose of writing poetry for children, who are supposed to be the future of our nation and of the humankind, is to achieve some such effects. Sar Po concludes, the purposes of reading and writing children's poetry is "One, to help children recognize and use more vocabulary so as to make their vocabulary more lively and down-to-earth; two, to breed children's innocent mind so as to make them purer and more lovable; three, to foster children's imagination so as to be concerned with things surrounding themselves, their homes and their communities; four, to implant in them senses of compassion so as to be good citizens in the future; five, to enhance their knowledge and educate them to their interest in aesthetics and mores so as to help increase their interest and happiness in life; six, to help them grow interested in arts and literature; seven, to guide children's mind and emotions on the right track of their life; and eight, to help them write poetry. Being able to write their own poetry, children would, consciously and unconsciously, establish their cognition of the value and meaning of life and its existence so as to be able to grasp the ideals of life." It seems to me that Sar Po's thesis is good and thoughtful, but there should be more: education to love the country, to love the people, to love hard work, and to love science. Sar Po's and my ideas of education achieved through children's poetry are different because of different political ideologies on the two sides of the Taiwan Strait.

I have three grandchildren. In addition to buying models of airplanes and vehicles, I also buy books of children's poetry. It seems to me that folk songs are strong in rationality and weak in children's interest. There are merits in folk songs. It is easy to chant folk songs of three-word, five-word and seven-word lines.

Sar Po's poetry is rich in children's interest and imagination. Its intention is to educate children in the areas of morality, intelligence and aesthetics. His poetry covers many things and is in everyday language. It is rhythmic and in the form of free verse. I read some poems to my grandchildren, Dongdong and Nannan. Their eyes were widely open at hearing my chanting of them:

"The River," "The river is like an intestine, / Peacefully squirming. / She does not eat much. / That is why she is always slim and long."

"The Waterfalls," "The distant mountain has waterfalls / Like a long towel. /

That is for the mountain to take a shower with."

"The White Clouds," "The white clouds are like cotton candies / Floating in the sky "and / Playing here and there and / Are then devoured by the sun."

Some of the vocabulary is difficult for the children, but, after being explained, the children immediately get to know it. Reading the poetry, children would learn more vocabulary. After hearing my chanting of the poetry, my grandchildren fell in love with it. I had to give the collection of the poetry to them.

Sar Po has won acclaims from the circle of children's literature. Some comment: "The tempo of his poetry is lively and rhythmic. His poetry is full of imagination which is innocent and interesting. There are images of the soul." Others say: "His poetry is able to grasp children's imagination and their ability to see things around them." Some of Taiwan's schools have adopted his poetry as supplementary reading materials.

Probably because Sar Po was writing children's poetry, he became sensitive to the conversation among his three children. "The crescent is like the white of a fingernail." "If you cut the mountains like a watermelon, you can cross them in your car." If you don't understand the child's mind, you will never recall your own child's mind. My grandchildren also have similar remarks in their everyday speeches, but I fail to keep a record of them.

Sar Po is thirteen years younger than I. He should be forty-six and he still keeps a child's mind. I do admire him here.

—The Hainan Newspaper, Mainland China, October 31, 1989.

童詩——人籟之最天真和最美妙的聲音　潘亞暾教授

兒童文學是孩子們的生活教科書、精神食糧，這個道理說起來大家都懂。然而，長期以來，兒童文學創作在海峽兩岸文壇並不受重視，名詩人"到來時發表幾首童詩應景是有的，而甘當辛勤的園丁，在兒童文學園地埋頭耕耘者就少見了。竊以爲，這跟許多文人潛意識裡那種"兒童文學是不登大雅之堂的小兒科"的觀念有關。所以，當我收到台灣牙醫師兼名詩人沙白寄贈的兩本童詩集《星星亮晶晶》、《星星愛童詩》時，感到特別高興。

重視兒童的教育和成長，就是重視祖國、民族的未來。沙白身爲名詩人，把創作健康有益的兒童讀物視爲義不容辭的社會責任，懷着一顆熱忱的愛心，多年來鍥而不舍，在報刊上發表了大量優秀童詩，這種努力、這份精神，最是難能可貴的。

在沙白看來："童詩是人籟之最天真和最美妙的聲音。童詩是人類心靈的搖籃。"（《星星亮晶晶》—自序）"兒童的心靈清新純潔，兒童對這個世界懷着無限的好奇、趣味和幻想，……童詩是捕捉兒童心靈的最佳語言文字的工具，也是展現兒童心靈的美麗繪畫和優美的歌聲。"我想,凡讀過沙白童詩的人,都會贊同他這種說法的。

《星星亮晶晶》和《星星愛童詩》薈集了沙白的童詩作品精華,裝幀精美,圖文並茂。這兩本童詩集我曾給很多學齡前兒童和小學低年級學生看過,他們都愛不釋手,在沙白創造的神奇的童詩世界中一個個流連忘返,迫使我看到:善良、純潔是兒童的天性,台灣、大陸乃至普天之下都一樣。沙白的詩是怎麼牽動孩子們心的?帶著這個問題,我把這兩本童詩集細讀了幾遍。我深感沙白確是一位洞察兒童心靈的詩人。他的童詩既富於兒童情趣,又蘊含著豐富的內容,幫助小讀者開闊眼界,拓展思路,領悟生活道理,形象思維和邏輯思維結合得很好,熔教育性、知識性、藝術性於一爐,實為童詩中的上品,在詩的構思、描寫、思想的提煉、形象的塑造和語言運用諸方面,都有獨到之處。

寓教於樂

沙白的童詩向小讀者們展示了豐富的生活畫面,用深入淺出的手法告訴孩子們應當如何生活、做人的道理。有些詩雖然写的是动物、植物或无生物，但实际上是在写孩子们生活中的思想、感情和事件，能引起小读者的共鸣、思考，使他们从中得到启发教育。《蚂蚁》这首诗中写道："因为你们是会咬人的害虫／我不盖房子给你们住／假如你们变为可爱的小蚕／我的房子就给你们住"表现了儿童爱善恶恨的心理。再请看《雷》"雷公在天上打起鼓来／轰隆轰隆地响／他不是在演戏，而是教人不要做坏事。"诗人以神奇的幻想塑造了一个具有社会属性的雷公形象，富于我国民间故事的传奇性。有的诗巧妙地运用比较手法，在批评讽刺反面形象的同时，歌颂、赞美正面形象，启发小读者分清美与丑、真与假、善与恶。《蜘蛛》这首诗写道："蜘蛛织的网是狡猾的陷阱／每天只等待小虫投入网中／当做你一个人吃的食物／而勤劳的可爱渔夫／却用鱼网打鱼给我们大家吃"。"蜘蛛"、"渔夫"二者的行为放在一起，互相对照映衬，赞美了一种不求索取、只求奉献的精神。这样的诗无疑能使小读者在思想情操上受到潜移默化的熏陶。

沙白抓住孩子们大都有理想、上进心强，但缺乏自制力的特征，用诗激发他们奋发上进。《树下读书》这首诗塑造了一棵挺拔的樹的形象，它"天天向上生長""天天在求進步""天天向下紮根"孩子們能從這棵充滿活力的樹上汲取追求進取的力量。

沙白童詩注意從道德品質、生活作風等方面對兒童進行教育，激發兒童的學習積極性、主動性，引導他們培養良好的習慣。詩集中有一些出色的惜時篇，如《鐘》："噹！噹！噹！/學校有個鐘/教我們要做好人"《時間》這首詩把時間比做天上的飛雲："飛去的是昨日/要來的是明日/而今日/就像我們釣到的魚/要好好地抓住/好好地珍惜/好好地料理"尤爲別致的是《鐘錶》："好鐘錶是最忠實的時間切割機/他將半天切成十二小時/一小時割成六十分/一分割成六十秒/不慌不忙/絕不投機取巧"這樣的詩既形象地介紹了時間的概念，又提醒孩子們要珍惜時間。《螢火蟲》是勸學篇中的代表作，詩中借螢火蟲的口説："書裡有光、有能、有知識/書裡的能比原子能強/書裡的知識比孔子、耶穌和釋迦多""學海無涯，必須要有求實精神，《棒球》這首詩"譏笑空心的水泡/只要風一吹/就消失了"詩中的形象鮮明而意味深長，富於感染力和説服力。在沙白看來，兒童養成良好的生活習慣是很重要的，他用《衣服》這首詩告訴孩子們："

衣服像樹木的花和葉子／一個沒有穿衣服的人／像落葉無花的樹木／難看又可憐／我們要像花開葉茂的樹木／穿著美觀整潔"這樣的詩想像豐富、形象生動、意味悠長，符合兒童獨特的思維方式，它所起的教育效果，我想是枯燥的說教所不能及的。

兒童並不是生活在真空中，沙白的詩從不同的角度反映了社會環境對兒童生活的深刻影響。《春天》這首詩以天真爛漫的童心，贊美人類間的互愛："所有的花木／同心協力／編織美麗的春天""所有的鳥兒／同聲唱出／春天美妙的歌曲""跳一跳歡樂的歌舞"詩中寫出了人與人之間美好高尚的道德情感。這是孩子們開卷得益的好詩，因為，誰都知道，對兒童進行愛的教育、愛的薰陶至關重要。集子中還有一些詩在樸素的形象中蘊含著哲理，給孩子們有益的啟示，請看《手指》："一隻手有五個兄弟／共同合作／從不分離""兩隻手有十個兄弟／大家合作／所向無敵"言淺意深，告訴孩子們，只有心齊了，才能把事情辦好。

兒童有旺盛的求知慾。沙白的童詩注意開闊孩子的眼界，啓發孩子們動腦筋，由已知到未知，由具體到抽象，在他們幼小的心靈裡播下愛科學、學科學的種子。

沙白善於抓住孩子們的好奇心，他的詩常常用形象的比喻和生動的事例，給孩子們啓思和思考。《颱風》這首詩寫道："天上沒有掛巨大的電風扇／爲什麼風吹得那麼大／吹得那麼響？／你沒有嘴巴／你沒有翅膀／爲什麼可以飛得那麼快？／吹得那麼響？"

詩中把颱風形象地比作"巨大的電風扇"，可謂大膽的想像。沙白常常通過兒童的眼睛和心靈去觀察、想像、認識、感受他們所接觸到的外界事物，例如，把蜻蜓比作一隻漂亮的小飛機，"請問你爲什麼的機器人"；把樹木比作造福世人的"萬能不必加汽油，也能飛得那麼久？"用生動的比喻和奇特的幻想，引導孩子們去揭開科學的奧秘，是沙白這類童詩的一大特色。

《湖》這首詩寫道："湖像一隻大眼睛／仰視奇妙的天空／而更奇妙的天空／是湖底綺麗的幻影"；《蠟燭》則觸類旁通，鼓勵孩子們去揭開大自然的秘密，詩中寫道："小小的針頭／可以麻醉獅子／小小的子彈／可以殺死大象／星星之火／可以燎原。"；《水》這首詩通過生活中的一些現象，形象地介紹了水的物理特性："水是多變的魔術師／放在杯裡，變成杯形/放在葫蘆裡，變成壺蘆形/在海裡變成海水/在河裡變成河水……"，把科學和詩有機結合，是沙白童詩的一個成功的嘗試，這些詩並非簡單的知識羅列，填鴨式的灌輸，而是注意運用形象思維，啓發孩子們開動腦筋，去探索科學世界的一些奧秘。

美的陶冶

沙白的詩對兒童的情緒、心理和思維方式有準確的把握，因而，他在創作中常常採用以虛帶實的方法，從現實生活出發，進行藝術虛構，使現實生活披上絢麗的幻想外衣，顯得更美、更浪漫、更適合兒童的欣賞趣味。

擬人、誇張、比喻、象徵，是沙白童詩中大量採用的手法。他的不少詩中運用擬人的手法。

根據兒童喜愛幻想的特點，他在一組描寫四季的童詩中，稱春天是個"魔術師"，夏天是個"頑童"，秋天是個亂丟黃葉的"畫家"。再看冬天的樹：《白天》寫道："太陽的眼睛一瞪/懶睡的大地都醒了"，冬天是個神奇的"伙夫"，有的穿淺綠的衣服/有的衣服被脫得光光/有的衣服將被脫光/有的穿着冷冷的冰雪白衣"

192

借助擬人手法，詩人把沒有生命的四季、太陽等變成有生命、有思想感情和有性格的人物。至於形象生動的比喻，更是俯拾皆是，例如，把太陽比作"大的電燈泡"，擔心它"別燒壞了"；把霧比作"烟"，"整個大地都在抽烟""那是給山洗澡用的"；把瀑布比作"一塊長長的毛巾"；把花園裡的花，比作"穿着美麗的衣服，做時裝表演"的"世界各國的漂亮小姐。"幾乎是生活中的任何事物，在詩人頭腦中都能產生奇妙的聯想：黑夜是"一塊巨大的黑布"，星星是"螢火蟲"，電燈是"能開黑夜的秘密的"鎖匙"，電話是最快速的"電動郵差"，溫度計是"感情豐富的升降機"，"最堅忍的朋友"，汽車是"不發脾氣的馬"，動物園是"動物的國際都市"，窗戶是"明亮的眼睛"，"門是房屋的嘴巴"，床像"母親的懷抱"，椅子像"牛背"……我很佩服沙白這種豐富的想像力，由此為他的童詩帶來了神奇的浪漫色彩和美的意境。沙白童詩中的環境，常常在一種虛擬的似真非真的狀態下出現，色彩明朗，氣氛柔和，既有神話般的情調，又有濃厚的生活氣息，字裡行間，維妙維肖地展示了兒童天真、活潑、幼稚的性格。

沙白童詩的語言生動風趣，活靈活現，娓娓動聽，富有詩情畫意，常通過兒童的口語、動作來表現他們豐富的內心活動，照顧到兒童的年齡、智力、興趣特點，沙白的童詩的語言，以淺顯、活潑、富於兒童生活情趣為主要特點，旨在引導學生進入更深層地擷取一些並非兒童常用的詞語，可謂用心良苦。此外，還運用了一些象聲詞，使作品更顯得意趣盎然。

我覺得，沙白的童詩下的定義是：〞具有兒童靈魂及兒童意識的詩。也就是在感覺和知覺上，對事物及其意象之表現，容易為兒童心靈感應的詩〞。他之所以熱衷於寫童詩，正是〞以自己的童心來和兒童作心靈的共鳴，並和兒童共享愉快有趣的、神聖的一刻〞。他在《星星亮晶晶》一詩集後附的《談兒童詩》的論文，有真知灼見。沙白的童詩便是他對自己理論的實踐。

沙白的童詩實在是孩子們的良師益友，而在我看來，若是
真正愛護孩子，就應當重視向他們提供有營養的精神食糧，這除了知識之外，還包括思想、情感、美育，以至自由的幻想。沙白對兒童詩不但對孩子們有益，對成年人也不無啓示，家長們看了這兩本童詩集，至少會意識到這樣一點，即

194

沒有純真的童心，沒有對孩子們發自內心的愛，是決對寫不出這麼美的童詩來的。（作者爲廣州暨南大學教授、台港澳及海外文學研究所主任）。

一九八九年10月下旬寫於暨南園

Children's Poetry

—The Most Lovely and the Most Innocent Voices of the Humankind.

Professor Pan Yatun (潘亞暾)

It is easy to understand that children's literature should be a textbook and intellectual food for children. For a long time, children's literature has been overlooked on the two sides of the Taiwan Strait. On Children's Day, some poets read their poems to celebrate the occasion, but they rarely write extensively on topics related to children. It seems to me that, for them, children's literature could not be of any importance. I was especially happy to have received two collections of children's poetry, Tinkle,Twinkle, Little Stars and The Stars Love Children's Poetry, from the dentist poet, Sar Po, from Taiwan.

To pay attention to children's growth and their education is to pay attention to the future of our country and our people. As a poet, Sar Po takes it as his social responsibility to create good and positive children's reading materials. It is commendable that he has had the warm heart and made great effort to ceaselessly publish children's poetry in magazines and newspapers over the past years. For Sar Po, "Children's poetry is the most innocent and the most wonderful voices for the humankind. Children's poetry is also a cradle of man's spirit." ("Preface," Tinkle,Twinkle, Little Stars.) With a fresh and pure mind, children are immensely interested and curious in the world around them. Language in children's poetry is the best instrument in capturing children's mind. It is also the best form to paint the beautiful pictures and to represent the melodious sounds of children's mind. Anyone who has read his poetry would agree to his remarks above.

The two collections of children's poetry, Tinkle,Twinkle, Little Stars and The

Stars Love Children's Poetry, contain Sar Po's best children's poetry. They are beautifully edited and bound with pictures in them. I asked some preschoolers and primary-school students to read them, and they like them much. They enjoyed being in the world created in the poetry by Sar Po. I was forced to see the virtuous and innocent nature of children in their reading of the poetry. I am of the opinion that children in Taiwan, Mainland China and other places should be the same. Indeed, I believe that Sar Po's poetry could touch the heart of children everywhere. I myself read the poetry more than once. I came to the conclusion that Sar Po is really capable of comprehending children's mind. His poetry is full of children's interest and varied images representing children's views of the world. The reading of the poetry would help the little readers see and form their ideas of their world so as to be able to learn to understand some principles of life. The goal is achieved through Sar Po's able management of ideas represented in poetic images and logics. The poetry is the best of its kind; the poetry has the functions of moral, intellectual and aesthetic education. The strong point of Sar Po's poetry lies in the fact that there is a good integration of poetic structure in proper language in closely knit narration and description of images representing ideas fit for children.

To Read Sar Po's Children's Poetry Is to Be Entertained.

He teaches the little readers how to be good citizens from their reading of his poetry which is full of vivid images described in language easily understood. To gain their resonant response, he employs plants, animals and inanimate things to represent children's thinking, emotions and events happening around them. In "The Ants," he writes, "You are such biting pests / That I would not build houses for you to live in. / If you are as lovable as silkworms, / I would build ones for you." Here, we see how children's love and hate could be represented. In "The Thunder," he writes, "Grandpa Thunder is beating the drum. / Boom, boom, boom! / He is not playacting. He is teaching us not to do bad things." Here, the poet is giving us an image of thunder according to folk culture in its socializing function. In "The Spider," he says, "The net woven by a spider is a tricky trap / Waiting for little worms to fall into it every day. / For you to eat, / The lovable and diligent fisherman / has to use a fishnet to catch fish." In "The Ox," Sar Po points out the virtues of giving and not asking for anything in return, or of alms-giving and dedication. Reading such poetry would move the little readers in their growth mentally and emotionally.

Sar Po writes poetry to urge children to actively move ahead in their pursuit of their ideals. In "Studying Under the Trees," he writes, "the trees are growing tall and upright" and "They are growing every day." "Their roots are also growing firmly downward every day."

Sar Po knows how to educate children through uplifting the quality of their senses of morality and of their life style. He urges them to learn positively and actively, guiding them to form good habits of life. There are some such poems as: In "The Clock," "Ding dong, ding dong. / There is a clock at school / urging us to be good students." In "Time," time is compared to the clouds in the sky: "Those that flew away were of yesterday. / And those to come belong to tomorrow. / Those with us today / Are like fish in our hand. / We should not let them go. / We have to grasp them firmly and cherish them and cook them well." In "The Watch," "A good watch is a cutting machine. / He cuts a half day into twelve hours, / One hour into sixty minutes, / And one minute into sixty seconds / Leisurely and correctly / And honestly." The poem shows the function of a watch and the nature of time. The poem teaches children the value of time and asks them not to waste it. The poem, "The Firefly," the poet urges children to study hard. Through the firefly, the speaker of the poem says, "There are light, power and knowledge in the book. / In the book, the light is brighter than the sun; / The power is stronger than an atomic bomb; / The knowledge is more than that of Confucius, Jesus Christ and the Buddha." There is unlimited learning. One has to do the learning little by little and step by step. In "The Baseball," "Bubbles empty inside / Would disappear / As soon as the wind blows." The image is clear and convincing. Sar Po thinks that it is important for children to form good living habits. The poem, "Clothing," tells them, "Clothing is like trees' flowers and leaves. / One who doesn't wear clothing / Would be like a tree without flowers and leaves. / It is ugly and pitiable. / We must be like trees with flowers and leaves. / We must be cleanly and beautifully dressed." Through the images and language of the poem, children are persuaded to do the same. The poet is not preaching; he is thinking in the shoes of children.

Children are not living in an isolated space from the rest of the world. From different angles, the poet is considering some aspects of social reality that would deeply affect their life. "Spring" praises sympathy and empathy among neighbors from the perspective of children:

All the trees and flowers
Work together
To knit the beautiful spring.

All the birds sing
In unison
The melodious songs of spring.

We the humankind of seventy billion souls
Must hand in hand be happily dancing and
Singing songs.

The poem describes the noble and virtuous emotions Sar Po wishes for the people in general. Children would benefit from the reading of the poem in the areas of love education and concern for others. Some philosophical ideas can be found in some everyday images as in "The fingers,"

> A hand has five brothers;
> They work together and
> Never separate.
>
> Two hands have ten brothers;
> They all work together and
> Are invincible.

The poem tells children to be cooperative with others in order to be successful in anything.

The Thesis of Intellectuality in the Poems.

Children have the desire to learn. Sar Po's poems help them to learn things unknown through those known and those abstract through those concrete. Reading the poems would bring children to their awareness of scientific ideas. Sar Po is good at grasping children's curiosity. He uses ordinary images to indicate something else. In "Typhoon," he says, "In the sky, there is not a gigantic electric fan, / Why is there powerful wind? / You don't have a mouth; / Nor have you wings. / Why can you fly so fast? / Why can you whistle so loudly?" To compare a typhoon to a gigantic electric fan is something unusual. Sar Po observes things around us through the eyes and mind of children. He records children's cognition, imagination and feeling about things out there. He compares trees to some omnipotent robots bringing bliss to us. He compares a dragonfly to a little beautiful airplane: "May I ask why you can fly for so long time / Without having to add gasoline?" He uses bold metaphors and images to reveal the secret of nature and science for children. In "The Lake," he writes: "The lake is like a huge eye / Reflecting the wondrous sky. / The wondrous sky is a beautiful phantom in the lake." The poem, "The Candle," helps children comprehend the secret of nature by analogy. In the poem,

> A little needle
> Can etherize a lion.
> A little bullet
> Can kill an elephant.
> A single spark
> Can start a prairie fire.

The poem, "Water," introduces some physical phenomena in our daily life.

> Water is like a changeable magician.
> Put it in a cup and it would take the shape of the cup.
> Put it in a gourd and it would take the shape of a gourd.
> Flowing in the sea, it becomes seawater, and
> In the river, it is part of river water.

It is an organic combination of science and poetry. This is not a simple listing of knowledge or cramming of it into children's mind. The poet uses the images in the poem to encourage children to deliberate the secret of nature.

The Thesis of Beauty in the Poems

In his poems, Sar Po takes control of children's mind, emotions and modes of thinking. He is good at guiding them to arrive at some abstract ideas through images of concrete things. So much so that ordinary things are cast in the mode of abstract images, which lead children to dig into the secret of the natural, scientific world.

The rhetoric techniques such as personification, hyperbole, metaphors, similes, and symbols are widely used in his poems. To satisfy children's desire for fantasy, the poet uses personification in many of his poems. He compares spring to a magician, summer to a wild cook, autumn to an urchin who litters yellow leaves, and winter to a magical painter. In "Broad Daylight," "As soon as the sun opens his eyes, / The earth gradually wakes up from her lazy sleep." Now look at trees in winter. "Some are in light green, / Others are stark naked, / Others would be naked, / And still others are loaded with white snow." Using personification, the poet offers life to the four seasons, projecting human emotions and characters onto the non-living elements. Furthermore, comparisons can be found everywhere. The sun is compared to a huge electric bulb which might burn out. The waterfalls are compared to "A long towel / For the mountains to take a bath with." Fog is compared to smoke: "The Great Earth is smoking. / As soon as Grandpa Sun wakes up, she stops." The flowers in the garden are compared to the clothes worn by the beauties from the world over in a fashion show. In the poems, anything ordinary can be shown in wonderful images. The black night is a huge black cloth. The electric light bulb is a key to open up the secret of the black night. The telephone is the fastest electric courier. The thermometer is an elevator of passion. The road is the most endurable friend. The zoo is a cosmopolitan city. The window is a bright eye. The door is the mouth of the house. The bed is like the mother's arms. The chair is like the back of an ox, etc. I admire Sar Po's power of imagination in his treatment of the common things in his poems. He gives new colors and images to them. He wants us to see things in the eyes of children, which shows their nature of being lively, naive, innocent.

Language in Sar Po's poems is of course lively and interesting. He is telling stories from children's intelligence. The language is easy to understand and able to express their emotions and feelings. Sometimes, he uses words beyond children's comprehension. Here, he wants them to learn more through reading of the poems. Furthermore, he uses onomatopoeia to enrich the images in the poems.

It seems to me that not only children but also adults can benefit from reading the poems. Parents would agree with me in that the poems would give something valuable, that is, spiritual nutrients, to their children. The poems would lead us to an imagined world not found in the real world.

Sar Po gives a definition to children's poetry: "Poetry that contains children's soul and consciousness. That is to say, representation of things and their images would emotionally and intelligently echos the spirit of children." He likes to write children's poetry because he enjoys sharing, through his undying child's mind, the holy and happy moment of children. "On Children's Poetry," an essay as a backword in Twinkle, Twinkle, Little Stars, discusses his theory and practice of children's poetry, and his insight in it.

It seems to me that Sar Po's poems could be a good teacher to children. A person without a child's mind or an intensive love for children would not be able to have written such poems.

— Professor Pan Yatun (潘亞暾), Director, the Graduate Institute of Taiwan, Hong Kong, Macao Affairs, andOverseas Literature, Jinan University, Guangzhou.

— Written at Jinan Yuan, October 1989.

浪亦難泯的童心：沙白〈海的吼聲〉略讀

／香港大學　余境熹教授

The Waves of the Sea Cannot Drown Children's Mind
—A Reading of Sar Po's "The Roars of the Sea"

　　沙白既能寫優秀的論文而與學界切磋，又能譜出一首首童詩，親近小孩子的心靈。其〈海的吼聲〉並非直接收進《星星亮晶晶》、《星星愛童詩》或《唱歌的河流》等童詩集內，但除成年讀者以外，該作在藝術和寓意方面，亦適合小朋友仔細品味，從而獲得啟發：

Sar Po wrote good essays discussing his ideas of poetry and of good children's poetry. His children's poetry appeals to many children. The poem, "The Roars of the Sea" is not included in his collections of children's poetry, Twinkle, Twinkle, Little Stars, Stars Love Children's Poetry, or Singing Rivers. It seems to me that the poem can be read by adults and children alike. Children can read the poem for its art and meaning. Children may read it and get enlightened in many ways:

The Roars of the Sea

海浪吼吼不停地拍著
向時間的擺動挑戰
看誰的旋律較美
誰的生命較長

The ceaseless beating of the roaring sea
Challenges the rhythmic swinging of time
To see whose melody would be more beautiful and
Who would last longer.

海浪吼吼不停地拍著
向太陽的輾動挑戰
看誰的體操高超
誰的體力較強

The ceaseless beating of the roaring sea
Challenges the rolling power of the sun
To see whose gymnastics would be better
And whose physique would be more energetic.

海浪吼吼不停地拍著
向大地的沉默挑戰
看看靜態較美
還是動態較美

The ceaseless beating of the roaring sea
Challenges the silence of the earth
To see whether being static is more beautiful
Or being dynamic is more beautiful.

海浪吼吼不停地拍著
原來他不訴說什麼
他只以吼吼不停的擊拍
來確立和炫耀他的身份和地位

Oh, I see. The ceaseless beating of the roaring sea
Does not want to prove anything.
She is merely ceaselessly beating and roaring
To establish and show off her identity and position.

—**The Large Ocean Poetry Quarterly, December 12. 1985.**

首先是語言。
First, let's discuss the language.

童詩不避重複，甚至常常以之增強節奏感，讀來琅琅上口之餘，亦方便兒童記誦和認字。例如，沙白《唱歌的河流》便收有〈我是一隻蠟燭〉，全篇分三節，每節均可見「我是一隻蠟燭 / 要燃燒熊熊的火光」之語;而沙白的〈河流〉重複「流」字，以及〈木馬〉的「木馬搖呀搖 / 木馬不會跑 / 木馬搖呀搖 / 愈搖愈逍遙」，刻意讓「搖」(遙)、「愈」、「木馬」複沓出現，配合疊韻的「逍遙」，皆是從細部加強節奏感的嘗試。

In children's poetry, repetition cannot be avoided. Repetition often enhances rhythm of the language. It is easier to read repetitive lines/words, and it is also easier for children to memorize them. In the following poem, the first two lines, "If I were a candle, / I would burn myself in great fire," in each stanza are repeated:

If I were a candle
If I were a candle,
I would burn myself in great fire
To give warmth to everybody and
To bring everybody hope.
If I were a candle,
I would burn myself in great fire
To drive away evil and
To bring kindness.
If I were a candle,
I would burn myself in great fire
To get rid of darkness and
To light up for others.

In the following poem, the word, "flow," appears many times:
The River

Water in the river flows
And flows.
Water in the river flows
Morning and
Evening.
It flows day and night.

The poem, "The Wooden Horse, reads as follows:

The wooden horse rocks back and forth.
The wooden horse cannot run away.
The wooden horse can only rock back and forth.
The more it rocks the happier it is.

The wooden horse rocks; yet it stays in place and seems to be happy. In the above examples, we find repetition gives rhythmic tempo of each poem.

在〈海的吼聲〉這篇，詩人不但以「海浪吼吼不停地拍著」為中心句，於每節開頭領起，像〈我是一隻蠟燭〉般；在詩的前三節，次句皆為「向□□的□□挑戰」，詞與詞的同位重複更能帶出和諧協調的節奏；而且，詩的首兩節全段對偶，複現的結構也能給人一定的熟悉感。在細節上，〈海的吼聲〉有著接近反復的「靜態較美」、「動態較美」，又有疊字的「看看」、「吼吼」，與〈河流〉、〈木馬〉相近，能夠增強全篇聲調諧協的效果。
　　其次是想像。

In the poem, "The Roars of the Sea," the line, "The ceaseless beating of the roaring sea," becomes the central motif. The same is also true in the line, "If I were a candle." The above two lines in the two poems create a reciprocating effect in their repetition. Their second line is both structured: "Challenging something" and "I would burn myself in great fire" to give a rhythmic tempo. In the poems, some overlapping terms reinforce a harmonious effect to them. In "The Roars of the Sea," the repetition of the structures of "To see whether being static is more beautiful / Or being dynamic is more beautiful" and "To see whose.../ And to see whose..." is similar to the repetition of some terms as in "The River" and "The Wooden Horse" They enhance the effect of the harmony of sound tuning.

沙白童詩之中，據事物特性來發揮想像力的精彩篇章甚多，例如《星星亮晶晶》的〈露〉：「露珠像情人的眼淚／向星星月亮／哭訴了一夜／等待太陽熱情的手／給她擦乾」，準確地以情人落淚、獲得安慰的故事片段，串連起露珠夜間生發、晨間蒸發的現象，熨帖自然，水到渠成；又如《星星愛童詩》的〈樹木〉：「舉起數十支手臂／展開數萬隻綠色手指／向太陽吸食光能營養／在春天裡搖首弄姿」，全詩以手臂喻樹枝，以手指喻樹葉，形象對應，易於聯想，而樹木在吸取足夠養分之後，「搖首弄姿」一語極能展現其生機盎然，且與樹冠、樹幹、枝葉在風中輕搖的畫面配合。

在〈海的吼聲〉裡，沙白表現出「海」的聲音（「吼吼」）、動作（「拍」岸）和起伏（「旋律」），還隱隱指出「海」的永恆特性（「誰的生命較長」），很好地捕捉住它的獨有形象。同時，作為配角的「太陽」像個車輪，沙白說它的位移為「輾動」；「大地」穩定、不變，像厚實木訥的人物，沙白則強調它的「沉默」和「靜態」——這些想像，都顯得奇特而精準，和見於〈露〉與〈樹木〉的巧思相當。還不止此，沙白更利用「輾動」來襯托「海」有著不相伯仲的活動能量（「體力」），又利用「沉默」來凸顯「海」的聲響與「動態」，使得讀者對「海」的認識更加立體。可以說，沙白對「太陽」、「大地」和「海」的形容各符其性，落墨甚準，在一篇之中，又能讓每個準確的形容互相勾連，為讀者呈現出一幅處處驚喜、極富想像力的美妙圖畫。

There are many poems by Sar Po where imagination is structured according to the characteristics of things. The poem, "Dew Drops," in Twinkle, Twinkle, Little Stars, reads:

Dew drops are like tears from a beloved.
She has been crying
To the moon and stars for a night and
Waiting for the warm hand of the sun
To wipe off her tears.

Here, the poet uses the technique of personification to characterize dew drops. The beloved's crying in tears and getting comfort from the sun fit in the process of nature. Furthermore, "Trees," in Stars Love Children's Poetry, reads:

They raise tens of hands
Pointing to the sky with thousands upon thousands of green fingers
To suck photosynthetic nutrition.
In spring, the waving of their fingers is like a young lady dancing.

Again, the technique of personification is used. Branches of the trees are compared to hands and leaves to fingers of a dancing young lady. After having sucked nutrition from the sun, the lady is so energetic that she begins to dance to celebrate the joy of life. Here, we see an image of the place of the trees vis-a-vis the heavenly bodies through the eye of children. In "The Roars of the Sea," motion and motionlessness are juxtaposed. The roaring sounds are produced by the eternally beating (dynamic) sea waves on the motionless (static) shores. The speaker of the poem asks, "Who would last longer?" This is a rhetorical question. The comparison of the rolling sun and the ceaseless beating of the sea against the motionless earth (shore) is the main theme of the poem. The speaker of the poem asks the rhetorical question. The answer is obvious: the dynamic and the static objects are equally powerful. Through the representation of them, the reader would form a sharp interpretation and imagination of them all in their positions in the cosmos.

最後是寓意。
Second, I would like to talk about implications in his poems.

沙白的〈談兒童詩〉說過,「成人寫的童詩,對兒童的心靈和詩想之啟發很重要」;身體力行,他所寫的童詩亦富含教育意義,常能為兒童貫輸正確的價值觀。舉例來說,在《唱歌的河流》中,〈一朵美麗的花〉叮囑兒童要,〈爸爸媽媽的皺紋〉促人勤奮讀書,《星星愛童詩》的〈時間〉則教導他們珍惜光陰——慈、孝、勤等美德,均藉由沙白之詩而進入童蒙之心。至於在〈鐘〉一篇,沙白更是直接喚醒兒童們「良知」的觀念。

In "On Children's Poetry," Sar Po argues, "The most important purpose for adults to write children's poetry is to enlighten the mind and the thoughts of children." His children poetry, which is educative, instills correct values for children. In "A Beautiful Flower," in Singing Rivers, the speaker of the poem advises children to love and take good care of grass and flowers. In "Father's and Mother's Wrinkles," children are encouraged to study hard. In "Time," in Stars Love Children's Poetry, they are taught to cherish time and practice values such as kindness, filial piety and diligence. The poem, "The Clock," helps children understand the importance of conscience.

回到〈海的吼聲〉，其教育意涵主要見於最後一段：「海浪吼吼不停地拍著 / 原來他不訴說什麼 / 他只以吼吼不停的擊拍 / 來確立和炫耀他的身份和地位」。在詩的首三節，「海」曾向「時間」、「太陽」和「大地」發起「挑戰」，這種上進的心態固然沒有不好；可是，「海」的「挑戰」原來缺少內涵，它只知重複「擊拍」，「吼吼」的聲響並無任何「訴說」的內容——如是者，「海」的舉動 不過就是自大傲慢的「炫耀」，趾高氣揚，卻不能獲得認同。兒童若然讀出此一訊息，則他們在努力尋求突破的成長路上，將更懂得「君子恥其言而過其行」，懂得「身份和地位」並不是靠大言炎炎即可攫得。由此觀之，〈海的吼聲〉和〈爸爸媽媽的皺紋〉、〈時間〉等篇一致，皆對兒童有著「心靈和詩想之啟發」。

Now, let's come back to "The Roars of the Sea." The lines in the last stanza can be as follows,

Oh, I see. The ceaseless beating of the roaring sea
Does not want to prove anything.
She is merely ceaselessly beating and roaring
To establish and show off her identity and position.

The educative value can be found here in the stanza. Having challenged time, the sun and the earth, the sea finally realizes that merely beating would not prove anything. In the above stanza, the sea comes to understanding that she could only prove her identity and position in the cosmos. Being oneself is the most important proof one could have gained in the order of things. The challenge would not change others. Only when one comes back to oneself and examines oneself can one understand oneself. The beating and roaring movement proves one's nature and position. Reading the poems, "The Roaring Sea," "Father's and Mother's Wrinkles" and "Time," children's mind and poetic thoughts could be enlightened.

略作補充——在〈海的吼聲〉中,「輾動」、「炫耀」等或許並不能算是童稚皆曉的詞語,但我認為誠如沙白所指:「有人覺得寫兒童詩,要用簡單的文字才好,因為兒童不懂得較專門性的和較深奧的語言和文字,我覺得並不盡然,因為任何學問都可以學習得來……所謂簡單或困難,只是有沒有去教,有沒有去學習而已」。〈海的吼聲〉適量地加入「輾動」等詞,若交給兒童去讀,讓他們有「去學習」的機會,則實際更有教育方面的助益。

One final word—in "The Roars of the Sea," vocabulary words such as "rolling power" and "showing off" may not be familiar to children. According to Sar Po,

"It is said that children's poetry should be written in simple language because children are not prepared to read complex and difficult language. I cast doubt on this point. Children can be trained to read it and take it as their own. If they are used to it through reading and training, they can use it in their own poetry writing.

Ours is an information society; children are exposed to all kinds of data in natural and social sciences. New ideas and language are there; children can take them as their own. There, they can learn and be trained to learn. A first-year student at a primary school, not having learned many Chinese words in kindergarten, learns some from the media. Children are taught to learn not only some words but also some knowledge of natural and social sciences. Teaching them to learn to know some language and facts about the world would solve the problem of simplicity and complexity of language. In short, if we teach children to learn, they would be able to use words and knowledge to read and write their own poetry."

It seems to me that in "The Roars of the Sea," vocabulary new to children is used for them to learn words and phrases with which they are normally unfamiliar.

爸爸媽媽的皺紋

沙白 詞
楊兆禎 曲

充滿親情地

爸爸的皺紋是賺錢的痕跡,媽媽的皺紋是燒飯洗衣的痕跡。

我沒有皺紋,因為我不會賺錢、燒飯洗衣;

我只会讀書,我要用書壓平爸媽的皺紋。

作者 簡介

- 沙白，本名涂秀田，一九四四年生，台灣省屏東縣人。屏東初中，台北建國高中畢業，高雄醫學院畢業，日本國立東京大學研究。

- 沙白自幼年即習中國古典文學，青少年時，更吸取西洋文學和日本文學等，而成為融合中西文學思想的詩人。

- 曾任現代詩頁月刊主編，阿米巴詩社社長，南杏社長，笠詩社社務委員，心臟詩社社長，布穀鳥詩社同仁，高雄市文藝夏令營講師，亞洲詩人大會和世界詩人大會籌備委員。

- 曾應邀參加一九八六年漢城亞洲詩人大會，一九八八年台中亞洲詩人大會，和一九八八年第十屆曼谷世界詩人大會發表論文〈詩是現代社會最重要的空氣〉，獲大會極高評價，曼谷英文大報THE NATION（國民報）以首頁引介此文。一九九〇年長沙世界華文兒童文學會議，艾青作品國際學術研討會。

- 曾獲中華民國新詩學會詩運獎、朗誦詩獎、高雄市詩歌創作獎、高雄市文藝獎、中華民國兒童文學會獎入圍（第二名獎）、心臟詩獎、柔蘭獎、亞洲詩人大會感謝狀、高雄市牙醫師公會和中華民國牙醫師公會感謝獎、台灣文學家牛津獎候選人。

- 現任臺一社發行人、《大海洋》詩社社長、中國文藝協會會員、中華民國新詩學會候補監事、世界詩人會會員、世界華人詩人協創會理事、中華民

- 國兒童文學會會員、台灣省兒童文學會會員、高雄市兒童文學寫作學會理事長、六堆雜誌編委、中華民國牙醫師公會編委。
- 著作：詩集『河品』、詩集『太陽的流聲』、中英文詩集『空洞的貝殼』（余光中、陳靖奇譯）、童詩集『星星亮晶晶』、『星星愛童詩』、童詩集『唱歌的河流』（中華民國兒童文學會獎入圍）、『沙白散文集』、『沙白詩文集』、傳記『不死鳥田中角榮』、『毛澤東隱蹤之謎（補著）』、『牙科知識』、『快樂的牙齒』等，以及T.S艾略特和保羅、梵樂希等英日文學之翻譯和介紹。作品曾被翻譯為英、日、韓文等，在外國及中國大陸曾介紹過。
- 留美：哈佛大學、波士頓大學植牙中心。
- 中華民國口腔植體醫學會專科醫師、台灣牙醫植體醫學會專科醫師、國際口腔植牙專科醫師學會院士、前中華民國口腔植體醫學會監事及專科醫師甄審委員、美國矯正學會會員。
- 國際詩人獎、榮譽文學博士、ABI及IBC國際傑出名人獎、美國文化協會國際和平獎；曾獲兩次國際植牙會議論文第二名獎。
- 沙白詩作列入韓國慈山李相斐博士出版的「現代世界代表詩人選集」。
- 現職：台立牙科診所院長
- 住址：高雄市新興區仁愛一街二二八號
 高雄市前金區中華三路一三五路
- 電話：（〇七）二三六七六〇三
- 手機：〇九一九一八〇八七五
- e-mail：shiutientu@msa.hinet.net
- e-mail：taiyi.implant@gmail.com
- 網址：www.taili-dentist.com.tw
- 郵政劃撥：04596534涂秀田帳戶

An Introduction to Tu Shiu-tien (Sar Po)

Born on July 28, 1944 at Toulun Village, Zhutian Township, Pingdong County, Taiwan Province, Republic ofChina.

Education:

Zhutian Primary School, Pingdong;
Provincial Pingdong Middle School;
Jianguo High School, Taipei;
Department of Dentistry, Kaohsiung Medical College.

Foreign institutions where he pursued further studies and research:

Research Institute of Dentistry, National University of Tokyo;
Osaka University of Dentistry;
National University of Osaka;
Research Institute of Dentistry, Harvard University;
Center for Dental Implantation, Boston University.

Interests :

Chinese classics, Western literature, Japanese literature. Oriental and Occidental philosophy and Thoughts on the Arts and their theory.

Honors and Awards :

Award for Writing of Poetry, Kaohsiung.
Award for Chanting of Poetry, Kaohsiung.
Award for the Arts and Literature, Kaohsiung.
Roelan Award, Kaohsiung.
Award from the Society of Cardiology.
Award from the Republic of China Association of New Poetry.
Outstanding prizes from International Poets' Association, ABI (American Biographical Institute) and IBC (International Biographical Center).
Award from the International Society of Poets

A certificate of an academician in the Association of International Dental Implantation Specialists at the University of New York.
Honorary Degree of Doctor of Literature (Litt. D.)
Outstanding People of the 20th-century American Biographical Institute (ABI) and the International Biographical Center (IBC)
Award from the American Cultural Agency for Promotion of World Peace.
Second Award in the presentation of a paper at the International Congress of Oral Implantologists (ICOI), twice.
2004 International Peace Prize, for outstanding achievement to the good of society as a whole, by the authority of the United Cultural Convention sitting in the United States of America.
2005 as one of the Top 100 Writers in Poetry and Literature, witnessed by the Officers of the International Biographical Center at its Headquarters in Cambridge, England.
2005 Lifetime of Achievement One Hundred, signed at the Headquarter of the International Biographical Center of Cambridge, England.

Current Occupation :

Dentist, Taiyi Dental Clinic and Taiyi Dental Implantation Center.

Associations :

President, the Amoeba Poetical Association, Kaohsiung Medical College.
Editor-in-Chief, the Modern Poetry Monthly,
President, the Nanxing Magazine,
President, the Big Ocean Association of Poetry;
A committee member for general affairs, the Li Journal of Poetry;
A lecturer, Kaohsiung Summer Camp;
Associate convener, the section of poetry, Kaohsiung Qingxi Association of the Arts;
Supervisor, the Southern Branch, the Chinese Association of the Arts and Literature;
An editor, the Liudui Magazine;
A preparatory Committee Member, the Asian Poet Conference;
A committee member, the World Olympic Association of Poetry;
An academician, College of World Culture;
Honorary Doctor, World Conference of the Poets.

Classification of His Works:

Collections of Poetry:

Hepin (So. The Streams), Preface by Zhu Chendong, "The Realm of Poetry—a Discussion of Sar Po's Poetry." Taipei: Modern Poetry Club, March 1966.

The Spiritual Sea. Kaohsiung: Taiyi She, September 1990.

The Hollow Shells, with Chinese and English texts, tr. by Yu Guangzhong and Ching-chi Chen. Kaohsiung: Taiyi She, December 1990.

The Streaming Voices of the Sun, in the Collection of Taiwanese Poets, #18, ed. the Li Journal of Poetry. Kaohsiung: Chunhui Publishing Co., November 2019.

Essays on His Poetics:

Sar Po's Essays on His Poetics. Kaohsiung: Chunhui Publishing Co., August 2020.

Prose:

Sar Po's Essays. Taipei: Linbai Publishing Co., September 1988.

Children's Literature:

「星星亮晶晶」Twinkle, Twinkle, Little Stars. Kaohsiung: Taiyi She, October 1986.
「星星愛童詩」Stars Love Children's Poetry. Kaohsiung: Taiyi She, September 1987.
「唱歌的河流」Singing Rivers. Kaohsiung: Taiyi She, September 1990.

Biography :

An Undying Bird, Tanaka Kakuei (不死鳥田中角榮). (In serialization, Taiwan Times.) Tainan: Xibei Publishing Co., May 1984.

Books on Dental Hygiene :

Knowledge on Dentistry. Kaohsiung: Taiyi She, August 1987.
The Happy Teeth. Taizhong: The Commission of Education, Taiwan Provincial Government, April 1993.

Translation of Texts and Theories of literature, Taiwan and Overseas:

"T.S. Eliot, 'The Dirty Salvages'", from English into Chinese, in Sar Po's Essays on His Poetics, pp. 256-273.
"Paul Valery's Literary Theory, One." in Sar Po's Essays on His Poetics, pp. 280-285.
"Paul Valery's Literary Theory, Two." in Sar Po's Essays on His Poetics, pp. 286-294.
"Paul Valery's Literary Theory, Three." in Sar Po's Essays on His Poetics, pp. 295-299.
"Paul Valery's Literary Theory, Four." in Sar Po's Essays on His Poetics, pp. 300-307.
"Paul Valery's Literary Theory, Five." in Sar Po's Essays on His Poetics, pp. 308-312.
"Paul Valery's Literary Theory, Six." in Sar Po's Essays on His Poetics, pp. 313-317.
"Paul Valery's Literary Theory, Seven." in Sar Po's Essays on His Poetics, pp. 318-325.
"On Something about Charles Baudelaire" by Kuritsu Norio, in Sar Po's Essays on His Poetics, pp. 326-336.

"On Charles Baudelaire" by Kuritsu Norio, in Sar Po's Essays on His Poetics, pp. 337-350-349.
"On Charles Baudelaire and His Poetical Language" by Kuritsu Norio, in Sar Po's Essays on His Poetics, pp.350-360.
"On Charles Baudelaire and His Prose" by Kuritsu Norio, in Sar Po's Essays on His Poetics, pp. 361-370.
"On the Pains of Charles Baudelaire" by Kuritsu Norio, in Sar Po's Essays on His Poetics, pp. 371-374.
"On Rambo" by Kuritsu Norio, in Sar Po's Essays on His Poetics, pp. 375-382.
"A Dream Inside and Out, Two Poems," by Shinkawa Kasue, in Sar Po's Essays on His Poetics, pp. 432-433.
"Two Poems by Yamamura Bocho," in Sar Po's Essays on His Poetics, pp. 436-437.
"Some Ideas on Taiwan Poets" by Kaneko Hideo, in Sar Po's Essays on His Poetics, pp. 438-439.
"Kawada Kakuei, Mushanokoji Saneatsu, Chen Tingshi," in Sar Po's Essays on His Poetics.
Papers Read in Conferences:

Papers read at the International Conference for Dental Implantation; Presented twice and awarded twice.
"Poetry Is the Most Important Air in Our Modern Society," read at the World Poets' Congress, Bangkok, Thailand, 1988; the speech was published in *The Nation*, Bangkok, Tailand.

譯者 簡介

◼ 陳靖奇

- ◼ 出生：台灣省雲林縣古坑鄉。
- ◼ 幼兒園：雲林縣斗六糖廠附設幼兒園。
- ◼ 國小：雲林縣古坑國民小學。
  台北市西門國民小學。
- ◼ 初中：台北建國中學。
- ◼ 高中：台北成功中學。
- ◼ 學士：國立臺灣師範大學英語學系。
- ◼ 碩士：國立臺灣師範大學英語研究所。
- ◼ 博士：美國明尼蘇達大學美國研究所。
  重點研究：美國文學與文化，「二十世紀三零時代的美國左翼文學，普羅大眾與資本社會的矛盾等議題。」

- ◼ 經歷：
  台北市立景美女子高級中學英語科教師。
  私立大同工學院講師。
  國立高雄師範大學教授兼夜間部主任。
  國立高雄師範大學教授兼英語學系主任。
  國立高雄師範大學教授兼英語研究所所長。
  國立高雄師範大學教授兼文學院院長。
  國立空中大學高雄學習中心主任。
  私立和春技術學院教授兼副校長。
  私立致遠管理學院教授兼應用英語學系主任。

Translated by Prof. Ching-chi Chen, Ph.d.

- Born at Gukeng, Yunlin, Taiwan, Republic of China.

▣ Educated:

- B.A. and M.A., National Taiwan Normal University, majoring in English.

- Ph.D., University of Minnesota, U.S.A., majoring in American studies (social sciences about America and American literature).

▣ Positions held:

- Professor of English, Department of English, National Kaohsiung Normal University.

- Chairperson, the Department of English, National Kaohsiung Normal University.

- Dean, College of the Liberal Arts, National Kaohsiung Normal University.

- Vice President, Hochun Institute of Technology at Daliao, Kaohsiung.

家圖書館出版品預行編目(CIP)資料

唱歌的河流 = Singing Rivers / 沙白著；
　莊敏蓉,劉淑威,張俊成,秦麗美,許博文圖；
　陳靖奇譯. -- 二版. -- 高雄市：台一社，
　民110.09
　　面；　公分
　中英對照
　ISBN 978-626-95122-3-2 (平裝)
863.598　　　　　　　　110015157

Original Chinese text by Sar Po
Translated by Ching-chi Chen, Ph.d.
Published by Shiu-tien Tu
Chinese and English texts copyright 2021 by Shiu-tien Tu
ALL RIGHTS RESERVED

唱歌的河流
Singing Rivers

（中華民國兒童文學會獎入圍）

著　　者：沙白 Sar Po
翻　　譯：陳靖奇 Ching-chi Chen, Ph.d.
發 行 人：涂秀田
出　　版：台一社
發 行 所：800高雄市新興區仁愛一街228號
電　　話：886-7-2367603; 886-9-19180875
印　　刷：德昌印刷廠股份有限公司
電　　話：886-7-3831238
郵政劃撥：04596534 涂秀田帳戶
登 記 證：行政院新聞局局版業字第4771號
中華民國七十九年九月十日初版
中華民國一一〇年九月十五日二版
Email：shiutientu@gmail.com
　　　：taiyi.implant@msa.hinet.net
WWW：TAIYI.egolife.com
　　　：taili-dentist.com.tw

版權所有・翻印必究　　定價新台幣400元(美金20元)